Secret Love

In the Beginning

Not even feeling guilty was going to make them stop.

LaShane Moore

This is a fictional book, all a product of the author's imagination. However, the situations that take place in the book happen in today's society. Any resemblance to actual events or persons living or dead is coincidental.

Warning: Adult Content. This is a story of erotic fiction and is for adult readers only. The book contains substantial sexually explicit scenes and graphic language.

MOOREHOUSE BOOKS

www.moorehousebooks.com

Cover design by Senir Design. Contact information- info@senirdesign.com.

ISBN # 978-0-9986208-1-7

Printed in the United States of America.

Thank you to my Father God,
for He keeps blessing me.

Acknowledgements

My life has taken me through so many distractions. But, I've found ways to lead myself back on the right track that God wants me to be on each and every time. Without Him, I wouldn't have found my way. It's been hard, but I have made it. I give Him the highest praise- all day, every day- for bringing me through and out of all situations.

To my four blessings: Bryant Jr., Brandon, Daijah and Derrick Jr., all I can say is you four are Mommy's blessings. When I do whatever it may be, I do it for you. I would say for us, but when I do whatever it is I do to make it to the next higher step, I think of your four faces and about how I can improve for you. Mommy loves you guys so much. Thank you so very much for understanding the nights Mommy couldn't join our family nights in our family room, because I was too busy typing or writing my book. I really appreciate all of you.

To my family, I thank you for the love, support, encouragement, and the blessings for my success. Writing books has been a very big blessing for me, to keep me humble through the troubled periods in my life, to find myself, and to provide ways to still help others through my writing.

To my mother and father for giving me life. If it were not for you both, I wouldn't be here. I thank you, and I love you both.

To my mother Sylvia for all the love and support that you

always give me, the encouragement to pursue my dreams, and for the constructive criticism too. Mom, I love you, and I thank you for helping choose the book cover.

To my dad, Mr. Hollywood himself, and to my step-mom Tori. I love you both, and I thank you for all your support.

To my brothers Jay and little Jerry whom I love so dearly with all my heart. Jay, I thank you for always believing in your sister and for always being there for me no matter what. Jay, as you would say, "And you do know that."

To my besties: Taisha and Tasha. Thank you for those nights when I read to you both different parts of my book, so you could tell me your thoughts of certain parts in different chapters. I enjoyed hearing your constructive criticism and then your anxiousness of wanting me to hurry up and finish my book, so you could have something to read. Well ladies, I'm finally finished. Now, you can start reading (smile).

To the rest of my friends, I thank you for the love, support, and the blessings for my success in my book writing and sales.

Thank you to my readers for your assistance during the creation of it, especially Dominique. I was able to see your enjoyment and enthusiasm for my book. Thanks for the praise you gave, while I took over your register, so you could read my book when we were supposed to have been working. That really did a lot for me. I thank you again.

I also want to thank Senir for designing my book cover and making sure it was just what I wanted. It's amazingly beautiful, and I thank you.

Last, but not least, to my publisher Dr. C. White-Elliott for all your hard work on my behalf for my book and for seeing my vision and challenging my strengths. With your help, I know we can turn this book into a bestseller. I'm so grateful to have you working with me.

Introduction

Five years ago, Katrina couldn't keep her eyes off Gary who always had a smile on his face or was laughing about something with his boys. None of the other girls in ninth grade were able to keep their eyes off him neither. But, something about Katrina made her stick out over everyone else to him. When he finally paid attention, he saw no one but her through hundreds of others.

When they first introduced themselves, they kept each other from laughing with their interesting conversations. Back then, he was the only fifteen-year boy with a deep voice.

Now at twenty-five years old, Katrina has everything any woman could ask for: a big lovely home in the suburbs of Los Angeles, a fancy car and truck, and a loving husband named Gary, who was her high school sweetheart. She knew he was the one back in school. Not only did they see it, but the whole school that voted them 'best couple of the year' their freshman year and every year after that saw it too.

While having it all, she still felt incomplete. A baby is what she wanted, and they have been working at it almost three times a day since they said "I do."

Prologue

It felt like everything for Gary was crashing down with his sales. Once again, his wife Katrina was right there to pick up the pieces, by getting more clients. Katrina proved to be a better at getting houses sold than her husband. She was bringing in extra income for their household. But, the extra work she put in was making her even more tired when she arrived home.

Even when Gary's days had been just as long as Katrina's, he still wanted some. It wasn't a night when he didn't want it. He just wanted to come home and get some, eat and watch football or a good movie. Even on his off days, he just wanted to wake up getting some from his wife who hadn't touched him the way he was used to in over a month now. He wanted it so badly, so he kept begging for it. So, she finally gave in. He had been planning in his head how he was going to smack her and flip her in the bed and how he was going to have her legs wrapped around his neck.

After a month of waiting, he knew he could go all night, but that wasn't the case: he came too fast. He told himself he was going to try again tomorrow, but that time he was going to try and go for hours.

He made a candlelight dinner for Katrina at their dining room table, but when she got home from work, she was beat and ready to dive into bed. She was really tired. She was only able to eat a little of her salad, a few bites of her steak, and half of her baked potato he had fixed up very nicely. However, she could never figure out why he would do that on the day she got home late instead of just coming to her and seeing what day she would be off for the week.

He had let her slide a few nights of not giving him any. But a few nights later, he had tried asking again. He definitely was not about to keep waiting a month at a time to have intercourse.

"Hey, baby can your husband get some loving tonight," he asked.

Lying down in bed next to him she whispered to him, "Babe, I'm tired. I've been selling houses all day, and I have another client at eight in the morning." "Please, Katrina? You said the same thing the other night and the week before; can I just get a little bit?" he asked with his firm deep voice. Katrina responded, "Not tonight, babe." She turned over and fell back to sleep.

As Gary lay there staring over at her laying there, he was a bit irritated with her. Working long hours at the office, she hadn't been on her wifely duties providing him with his sexual pleasures on a regular lately. That night, just like many other nights lately, he was left up to using his hand, before falling asleep. He was very agitated from not getting any on a regular; he was missing making love to his wife every night. But on nights when she did, it was so amazing. He just wished he could start back getting it every night like he had for many years. Although he was becoming used to not being intimate every night lately, he didn't want to get used to it. But Katrina really left him no other choice.

Chapter 1

The Move In

Katrina had a problem with a woman who was being a little too friendly with her husband. She didn't care if the woman knew him or not. Nor did she care if the woman had known him for a long time. All she knew was the woman needed to keep her hands off her husband. If anyone was paying attention, the woman had rubbed Katrina the wrong way, but Katrina knew after that night the woman would never see him again.

Luckily for him, it was his mother Joann's retirement party. Otherwise, Katrina would have turned the place out. She noticed how his look showed he did not remember who the woman was. As the woman threw out a few hints, Gary placed his finger on his chin with his eyes scrunched. Then, it came to him. "Oh yeah. Now, I remember."

After they had talked and reminisced for five minutes, he finally introduced Katrina as his wife to the woman. Katrina smiled at her and spoke to her, but she was still pissed at Gary. He had never done that before. She gazed at his mother and then at his father, then back at her husband and then again at the woman. His mother and dad sat there seeing no problem with it. They never said anything; they just sat there conversing with others at the table. But, Katrina had a problem with it. So, she excused herself from the table, and Gary followed. Gary and Katrina went and stood off to the side against a wall drinking their wine where they were able to talk in private.

"I'm letting you know what just happened over there was very disrespectful."

"Babe, I'm sorry. I didn't know how to tell her to stop touching me without being disrespectful." Katrina stared at him and did not say a word. "Babe, you can forgive me right?"

"Yes, Gary, but don't let that shit happen again." There was no need to hold a grudge about it as long as she had told him how she felt and the fact he better not do that shit again.

Soon, it was time for the speeches. It was a very large crowd. Katrina waited until all the speeches to Gary's mom were made from other teachers she worked with and her boss who also spoke. She wanted to give them a business card.

"Well, I guess I'll go mingle," she told Gary. "You know- pass out these cards to get more potential clients."

"Go ahead. Don't let me hold you."

Katrina handed her empty glass to the waiter who was just walking over to them and grabbed a new glass of wine from the tray she was holding. Then, Katrina walked off. She walked around the entire room to every table and handed her business card to each and every guest, letting them know when they were ready to buy a home, she could help them. Gary didn't budge. He stayed there drinking his wine, while she walked around. She glanced at him from across the room and saw him get another glass from the bar.

His ass should be the one passing out business cards, not over there drinking, she thought. Katrina looked around to make sure she didn't miss anyone. She loved what she did, and she tried to hand out at least fifty cards a day. She always knew one or two of the fifty would call, sometimes even more. It brought satisfaction to Katrina to know she could bring down stress and give relief to whoever found their financial situation overwhelming from not being able to buy a home.

She helped her clients clear up their credit, and she taught them ways to build their credit, so they could be prepared when they were ready. Everywhere she went, she was always business minded.

While Gary was still at the bar, his dad walked over and got a drink too. Gary talked to his dad about what happened at the table, what he obviously didn't pay any attention to, and how it bothered Katrina. His dad quietly listened to his son talk.

The only advice he could give was to let him know, "In public, you must respect your wife at all times, or you will be in the dog house for sure." Gary kept going on and on about how mad Katrina was. His dad stopped him and told him not to beat himself up about it. What's done was done, and there was nothing he could do about it.

After Katrina was done, she joined Gary at the bar. Before

taking a seat on the bar stool, she leaned towards him giving him a kiss on his lips. Gary then apologized to his wife for what Maxine did at the table. Katrina looked at him and stared.

"Babe, would you like for me to order you a drink, or do you want more wine?" Gary asked her.

"Do you think I'm going to forgive you for a drink?" she asked with a smile.

"Babe, come on? I said I was sorry for that."

Katrina looked at the glass that was in front of him. "What's that you're drinking?" she asked.

"Patron."

"Umm," she hummed. "Maybe not patron. I'll stick with the wine."

Gary called over one of the waiters who was walking with the trays. After one came over, Gary got a glass of wine for Katrina.

"So, babe you know all these people here?" Katrina asked him.

"Yeah, most of them from when I used to go up to my mom's job when I got out of school. Some even brought their kids to my birthday parties when I was younger."

"Oh, okay," she nodded her head.

Once Katrina began drinking her wine, she calmed down. She was fine and more talkative. Through all the many conversations Gary and Katrina had and the laughter they shared, she grew more at ease about being there because at first she was ready to go.

The more drinks they had made the evening that much better. They had fun, and the retirement party was a success and turned out great. The hotel was popular for such events. When they made it home, Gary tried to get him some because he knew Katrina was tipsy. But, she hit him with, "You're not off that easy, buddy. Remember what happened earlier."

"Katrina, I thought we already squashed that at the party," he told her. She took off her clothes and lay in bed naked. "You know you're wrong, right. I can't get none, but then you get in bed naked." She looked at him and smiled.

"Good night, Gary."

"Good night," he said, and then he lay there. He wrapped his arm around her trying to leave a space in between them, and then he too fell asleep. Katrina slept peacefully, until she was awakened by the non-stop ringing of her phone. As she looked for her phone on her nightstand next to her bed, it rang continuously. She silently wished whoever it was would hang up. As she looked for her phone that she didn't feel like answering, it was ringing for the fourth time.

"Gosh! Stop calling me!" she said as she continued to look for it. Katrina saw the flashing lights from her ringing phone over on her dresser. She got out the bed to get it. On her screen, it said, "Restricted." She hesitated to answer as she wondered who could be calling her that early.

Finally, after the sixth ring, she answered with her sleepy voice. It was her baby sister Brandy. Brandy was getting put out their parents' house at 5:00 in the morning. Brandy had called her sister to tell her their mom was putting her out and she wanted to see if she could come to live with Katrina and her husband, until she found her own place. Katrina just held the phone to her ear while shaking her head from side to side.

"Mom and Dad just put me out the house!" Brandy yelled.

"Brandy, I already heard you the first time you said it."

"Can I come stay there for a while until I get myself together?" she asked her sister.

"Yeah, of course," Katrina said before Brandy could finish her sentence. Katrina already knew how their parents were when she was living there. They were the reason she got married and quickly moved out.

As an adult living at home with her parents, it was like walking on eggshells to hear them complaining about everything from walking too loudly, talking too loudly, laughing too loudly, too much company, or even they would to say to her, "You're watching the T.V too loudly." She thought, *How could I have the T.V up too loudly if it is always at volume 15.* She knew just how her baby sister was feeling. The next day, Brandy didn't waste any time. Brandy packed all her stuff, moved out, and went to Katrina's house and moved in.

Just days later, Brandy was doing her laundry at the laundry mat. Katrina and Gary had both a washer and dryer, but Brandy didn't want to spend her Tuesday in the house all day washing clothes. She wanted to get everything done in a couple of hours.

Shortly afterward, she was interrupted by a nice-looking guy who introduced himself to her as Chris. He was really tall compared to her. He stood six feet tall, just how she liked her men. He had light brown skin with a low-cut fade nicely groomed with deep waves. She could tell he had good hair. She was only 5'3 herself. He was okay, but he didn't have huge muscles like she liked. He was not that big nor was he slim. She didn't like men to be too slim. Overall, he was cool.

They began talking, and they talked the whole time she was there, and then they exchanged numbers before leaving. After only three days of meeting him, Brandy wanted to bring him to the house, but because it was her sister's house, she at least wanted to respect her by asking permission and not just letting him pop up.

Once Katrina made it home from work, Brandy couldn't wait to see what her sister had to say in response to her request. When Katrina walked in from work, Brandy greeted her.

"Hey, hey sis. How was work?"

"Long and pretty busy, but good."

"That's right, being busy I bet made the day go by faster."

"Shit not fast enough," Katrina said.

"Ha, Ha," they both laughed.

"Hey, sis, I was wondering if I can invite a friend over?"

"A friend! Who is this friend?" Katrina asked. Brandy stood there just looking at her. "Who is this friend?" Katrina asked her again.

"Well, it's this guy I met three days ago when I went to go wash clothes at the laundry mat."

Katrina laughed, "Girl, your ass is crazy."

"No, he's cool though."

"Well, what do you even know about him, Brandy? You just don't meet somebody and bring him to where you live," Katrina said.

"Yeah, but he seems special and real cool."

"Brandy, you just don't get it."

"We're just going to hang out here and probably watch a movie."

"Okay, Brandy. I hope you're right about this guy."

"Katrina, it's Friday...I don't have a job."

"You say that to say what?" with a straight look on her face.

"We're just going to chill. That's all." Katrina was still looking at Brandy like she was crazy.

"Come on. It's the weekend. We can all hang out together and drink some beers. I could fry up some chicken. You can make your special seven-layered dip. We already have the tortilla chips. How does that sound?"

Katrina slowly nodded her head up and down.

"It'll be fun. So what do you say?"

"Okay, Brandy. I said okay."

Gary was cool with it, but little did they know he had not been able to keep his eyes off Brandy, his wife's little sister, since she moved in. It was something about her that made him stare at her all the time. Brandy saw his lustful stares. She didn't pay it any attention, and as far as telling her sister, she didn't say anything. He didn't know why he stared and thought nasty thoughts about her. It was not likely for any of it to ever happen for real. He was just straight tripping.

Brandy called Chris and invited him over. By the time he arrived, everything was set up nicely on the kitchen counter for them to all serve themselves. Everything had already been done for about an hour, but they waited on Chris, so they could all eat, watch the movie and start drinking at the same time.

Before the movie was over, Katrina and Gary were already in their bed, while Chris and Brandy stayed up watching the rest of the movie and didn't realize until after the movie was over how late it was.

Brandy assumed her sister and brother-in-law were sleeping. Actually, they were in there making love for the first time in six days after she got over that little situation that happened at the retirement party. Before that night, Gary was left to stroke himself while Katrina was asleep right beside him.

Gary was lost in his own sexual pleasure. He was trying to fulfill his own desires. He didn't care if Brandy's company was still over that night. After the two finished making love, Gary noticed how he exploded with full force of cum, but she didn't. He started thinking maybe she'd been sleeping with one of her clients while she was out showing houses. Maybe that's why she never had the time to fulfill his needs. After asking her about it, she got upset that he would even ask her that, and they both just went to sleep.

Later that night, Brandy told Chris because it was late he could spend the night, but he had to leave before her sister awakened in the morning. Happy like hell when she told him he could spend the night, he knew for sure it was about to be his lucky night.

It had been a very long time since Chris had got laid. From all the drinking they were doing, he was horny. Of course, he wasn't going to mention it first. He didn't want to come off as a jerk, but at any point when he felt like she was trying to offer it, he was planning on taking the offer. The movie was a comedy, so they continued to enjoy each other's company with laughter and more beers.

Brandy rubbed Chris's pants leg along with rubbing her arm against his arm every time she laughed. He noticed Brandy was very tipsy but that didn't stop her from drinking more. She didn't seem like she was an amateur, so he figured she could handle herself. He figured she should know just what she's doing. The more she kept on, he knew he was going to get some. Chris was sitting there becoming drunker and feeling very horny. He felt like he was about to burst any moment. He was already looking at her and sexing her with his eyes.

"Brandy, what time does your sister wake up?"

"On the weekend, she always sleeps in. She doesn't come out her room until about noon."

He looked at her like she was crazy. "Why so late?" he asked.

"Well, she works all week, and sometimes, she works really long hours, so on the weekends, she just sleeps in."

"Oh, okay. Why don't you ask your sister to hook you up with a job?"

"I have tried to see if she could get me plugged in to be her assistant or the person to find the buyers for her company, but she hasn't gotten back with me on that. It's cool. I love her anyway. I can go find my own job."

"Yeah, I guess you should."

They continued watching the comedy. After the comedy show was over, Brandy was already in bed sleeping with Chris on their first date. She didn't plan on sexing him yet, especially not in her sister's house. Well, at least not when she knew Katrina was right upstairs. Brandy was not trying to get put out again for the same shit. She was not trying to be homeless. She knew her sister didn't play. She knew Katrina wouldn't even think twice about putting her out.

Brandy had a 30-day rule of no sex, and that's if she ended up liking the person. She was really strict with her rule. She was only trying to be generous by letting Chris stay over, so he wouldn't have to drive home so late. Also, they had been drinking, and she didn't want him to get into an accident or get a ticket. As they lay together side by side sleeping, Chris appreciated the thought she had about his safety. He respected her for not wanting to do anything sexual as they had just met.

Sleeping soundly in their room, Katrina and Gary never knew Chris slept over that night. Brandy had gotten away with it, so she kept letting him stay over from time to time since that first time. However, in less than two weeks, an awkward situation took place.

Chris was over, and he and Gary were chilling on the couch

watching the game. Katrina was at work. Brandy was being a host to the two guys. She was flaunting back and forth from the couch to the kitchen bringing snacks and beer for them in her little pink dress. Sitting back, Gary was supposed to be watching TV, but his eyes couldn't help but to look at her as she walked back and forth. Brandy turned her head the other way when she noticed him watching her.

Later that night, Gary wanted some junk food to eat, but there was none, so he drove to the store to pick up snacks to munch on. While there at the store, he also picked up a three pack of condoms just in case if he got tempted to do something.

By that next morning, as he walked to the kitchen, Gary could no longer resist. His instant arousal told him what he needed. He knew it wasn't right but that one time real quick shouldn't hurt as long as she didn't tell anybody when she woke up and saw it was him. He tried to push his erection down, but it wouldn't stay down. *Fuck it. What the hell,* Gary mumbled to himself. He wanted to give it one more try. He tried again to contain his erection, but that still didn't work.

He had to place his hand into his pants to reposition his penis, which was rock hard. *Damn like that,* he thought. Just looking at her aroused him. He thought his penis was going to go down, but he was still rock hard. He was not planning on walking pass her again without getting what he wanted. Gary poured himself a glass of orange juice and stared at her asleep on the couch as he drank his juice. A moment later, he opened one of the cabinets, the one he hid the condoms in last night. He took a condom out the pack and threw the box back inside the cabinet. He ripped the wrapper open with his teeth and then he slid it on his penis. He walked out the kitchen and straight towards the couch. He pulled the cover up, and he saw Brandy only had a night gown on. He quietly slid in underneath the covers right behind her. Very slowly, he raised the back of her gown up and felt her butt area. He thought, *Damn, she's not wearing panties.* All he felt was her skin. He moved his hand to the center of her butt and that's when he felt a string. Brandy had on G-String. He slid the string from the center of her butt; then, he slid in his penis and began grabbing her by the hips, pulling her back into him. Her body felt so soft. He held on to her side firmly without letting go, and every time he arched back he went in deeper.

It didn't bother him that she was asleep still. But, just after a few pumps, she awakened with the sound of a moan. That morning, Gary had awakened with sex on his mind. Brandy thought she was dreaming the dream of her life, but it felt so real. She didn't want to awake from it. Then, she thought while her eyes were still closed that her sister had let Chris in right before she left for work.

After drinking a little bit too much with him last night, Brandy didn't remember if he had stayed the night. She didn't remember hearing a doorbell that morning. She didn't know what was going on; she felt like she was still out of it. Gary noticed she was waking up with her movements and her moans, but not even that stopped him. During the whole act, she never even turned around. As he continued gripping her body, he continued going in from behind. Gripping her breasts, he started going faster. He kept adjusting the speed from slow to fast.

Finally fully awake, Brandy asked, "What are you doing? Dammit, Chris!" Although it was feeling damn good, all she could think about was her 30-day rule. She felt it was too soon for what he was doing. She wasn't trying to break her 30-day rule with him. She didn't want him to get what he wanted and then not hear from him again. Attempting to ask the question again for the second time is when he pushed down in her deeper. It was a feeling she was not prepared for. The sound of her moan was his hint to keep going.

"Mmmmm....." she moaned.

It is feeling so good, she thought. Neither of the two wanted to part from each other's enjoyment, especially after making each other's toes curl, moan, and body dripping wet the way they were. Once her eyes opened all the way when they were done, she saw it wasn't her friend Chris. Her eyes got big......

It was Gary. Brandy didn't know how Gary could think he could just slide his dick inside her while she was asleep or just put it in her period for that matter. Gary couldn't resist that pink dress she had on yesterday looking just like his wife. Brandy couldn't believe her sister's husband had no shame. She wondered why her? Why would he choose her to have a fucking affair with?

Brandy had the body and the face, but Gary didn't care about the face, because his wife was beautiful too with a perfect body. He was more focused on Brandy's body. He wanted some of it. He was only thinking of himself and the sexual needs he was trying to fulfill.

"Why me, Gary?" Brandy asked him.

"Brandy, I was horny, and you were just lying there."

"But Gary, that still doesn't give you the right to do that to me," she told his ass.

"Well, you were lying on the couch bed. I was going into the kitchen to find something to eat before heading out for work, and all I saw was your body hanging halfway from under the covers. I instantly became aroused. It hardened so quickly from a glimpse of you. I couldn't take my attention off you, and I had too."

"Ain't that about a bitch! What do you mean you had too?"

It had only taken a brief glance before that loyal husband wasn't so loyal anymore. She couldn't believe he admitted that to her. Up until that moment with Brandy, he had not had sex in about a week. She made him remember just how incredible sex is, why he loves it as much as he does, and why he feels he needs it every day.

Brandy didn't know how to start or where to start telling him to leave her alone because all she was hearing were reasons why he did it, as if though it was okay. And she sure as hell didn't know how to tell Katrina. She knew she couldn't call it rape for the enjoyment she actually just had herself, as he woke up body parts that had not been active in a while. But, she was not about to tell him she enjoyed it, as he lay next to her pulling off his condom.

She just came out and said it, "Gary, you shouldn't have done that, and you can't do this ever again."

Her resistance meant nothing to him; it actually turned him on even more. Drained out and tired, he gave her a kiss on her nose and said, "Thank you." He got up from the bed to flush the condom down the toilet along with the wrapper to leave no evidence behind. He slipped his pants and T-shirt back on and whispered in Brandy's ear, "See you later."

As she began to fall back asleep, she thought, "A little quickie. I will keep quiet. I'm not trying to have my sister lose her mind and blame me for everything all for ten minutes of sex." When she had awakened again, she got up to use the bathroom. She was not able to hold her balance. It felt like he was still inside of her. He had her walking a bit differently. She went and took a shower and went on with her day.

Afterwards, Brandy didn't think any more about it. She blocked it out of her mind like it didn't happen. If only her sister knew what her husband had done with her earlier.

The next morning about the same time at 7:30, Brandy was laid out in a deep sleep. Gary was rock hard, and once again, Katrina left for work without pleasuring him. He was not trying to use his hand at all. Walking downstairs and down the hallway, he walked past the living room seeing if Brandy was still asleep. Gary walked passed playing it off and saw that she was.

He wanted to get her while she was asleep. At least, he wanted to try to before she tried to fight him off or make him stop. Gary was having the hardest time trying to resist her. He wanted to see how far he could get with her that day, hoping he could go all the way with it again. He lightly lifted up her covers and easily slid in bed right behind her again. He was already at attention down there, as he slid in the bed with his hand already holding it. He had good aim for her hole, so with his other hand, he lifted her butt cheek up to open her just a little. Then, he easily slid it inside of her from behind. She felt it heat her up inside. The feeling was so strong, and her body was open wide. The back and forth pumps against her butt woke her up.

"Gary, not again," she said.

"What is it, Brandy? You don't like it?" he asked her.

"I never said that, but you're my sister's husband!! You must want to die. If she finds out, she is going to kill us both."

While she was steadily talking, he was still going in with each thrust; he was grinding it in a circular motion. He was so into it that he just let her talk.

"I'm not scandalous. We never slept with each other's man before. We just don't do shit like that."

"Who's going to tell her? I'm not," he said. "Brandy! What are you afraid of?"

"H-E-L-L-O? My sister walking in on us and killing us both! The fact you're fucking me is not cool!"

He laughed at her with her snappy attitude trying to talk smart to him. He just laughed at her. He knew how she was, and he knew he could break her out of that in no time. Nothing she said he listened to. It was funny to him to hear her say the things she was saying, acting like she didn't want it as badly as he did.

"She won't be here for another five to six hours. This is our little secret. We're just having fun."

"Fun!! You mean you're having the fun," she said. "No, I didn't sign up for this Gary."

"Well, I think you like it too, Brandy. I don't remember you stopping me at any time yesterday."

"How could I? I was sleep remember."

She did not believe herself right then because she had given in twice already. She was starting to enjoy his company, but she kept that to herself. Her telling him to stop didn't sound too convincing. That's why when she told him to stop he kept going. He turned her over on her back, as he got on top of her while arching his back. He began going in and out of her slowly but deeply. With each thrust, she moaned with her eyes closed.

As he was pounding inside her, they were listening as her pussy was making loud farting noises. Shortly after, the position was changed while Brandy was still lying on her back. He began lifting her butt off the bed, raising her in the air with his arms underneath her lower thighs while he was inside her. They didn't stop until they both climaxed. It wasn't long before they did. *Oh boy* when they did, it felt like he was still inside. He put her straight to sleep before he left for work.

The next morning, there went Gary again. That time, Brandy was awake. He quickly stopped in his tracks because he knew because she was already awake she was not about to let anything go down. He was wrong. She was giving in. She was not only enjoying his company, but she was also enjoying all the sexual positions he put her in that she hadn't even experienced with Chris yet. He stood in front of her with no shirt on looking so damn handsome. He had on no pants and no boxers; he was ready for her.

Brandy said to him, "You're not going to come and slide in bed underneath these warm covers?" She lifted up her covers from the bed. He was caught by surprise that she was willing that time. She thought, *What the hell? He's already done it twice already.* Trying to ignore him since the first encounter didn't last long for her. As much as she didn't want to, she became attracted to him. He slid in bed with her kissing her romantically before putting her in the doggy-style position.

He had her just how he liked- legs spread out and butt propped up as he went in and out from behind, as she screamed his name. She really didn't know what it was about her that kept him wanting her. It started off as a little quickie that would just happen once, but ended up turning into casual sex. Unlike his wife, she didn't have many demands once she was with it. So with her, he could have it whenever he wanted it and go as deep as he wanted at any time. He just made sure he was protected by either wearing a condom or by pulling out when it was time to cum.

He was given the control he needed sexually without excuses and many questions, and that's what he liked. They tried to convince themselves that after that next time, they are going to stop sleeping with each other. But convincing each other didn't work. Day after day, he wanted it. He thought it was insane at first for wanting to do it when it was just a thought, but now that he had been doing it, he believed he was insane just for thinking it was insane. The feeling was so good or maybe even better each and every time; it was warm inside every time.

She lay with her head on top of the pillow as he was directly on top going in her. His eyes stared down at her, as they just gazed into each other's eyes. Their eyes spoke a lot of words without speaking with their mouths. As he could feel her now for the first time actually joining in with him as he continued positioning himself over her body, he took it that she wasn't afraid nor nervous any more as he slid in his hardened tip. Brandy liked it. She figured, *Okay, I'll give this one a pass. He better leave me alone now that I gave it up to him, without him having to sneak like before, before I have to marry his ass myself.*

He had her in a zone talking to herself out loud. She often sat and thought his ass was crazy. She didn't know what came over him. He never showed any interest before. All of sudden she moved in, and he thought he could have sex with both sisters. "I don't think so," she mumbled as she still spoke to herself.

With Gary, she found herself trying to tell her mind something differently. Brandy told him verbally more than once that she was not okay with what he did, but when it came down to it, she eventually became okay with it. She was with sexing in the washroom upstairs, against the wall downstairs in the dining room, to different parts of the house, and even on the floor. He couldn't stay still, but she held on for the ride. He wanted it every day. She felt kind of bad. She didn't know how she was going to stop it. Brandy figured maybe if she invited her friend Chris over more often maybe Gary would leave her alone.

When Chris came around, Gary really never had too much to say to him. She didn't know if he was jealous or not. She didn't know why he would be when he and her sister were married. Even though Gary just took it from her after two weeks, she stuck with her 30-day rule with Chris.

One day, Chris paid her a visit. She wore the dress he liked, giving him easy access to be able to slide his hands between her thighs massaging her center part. He brought over a bottle of wine for them to drink.

"Okay, just one glass for me."

"Okay," he smiled.

Before they knew it, they had drank the whole bottle. Brandy and Chris had spent another night together just watching comedy shows, laughing and eating snacks. It was fun; enjoyment was present between them all the time.

When the 30-day rule was up, Chris was happy Brandy let him stay the night until the next day. Only that time, she didn't make him leave. That morning when Katrina and Gary both left for work, the two sat up and gazed into each other's eyes. His warm touch when he touched her body made her tingly all over. She gave him a little more than just tongue action, which is what he was used to only getting from her.

Chris immediately felt a really close connection to her. After one long intimate hug and kiss, they knew that would lead into lovemaking. He whipped his penis out; he was happy that his thirty days of waiting was over. He stuck his penis inside her, and it felt real good going in. He knew just what to do with her that made neither of the two want to stop until they both exploded.

After he got some from her for his first time, he thought she was the most fantastic lover he had ever had. After that first time, they both felt the desire and wanted more. The feeling made Chris want to always feel that feeling for the rest of his life. Brandy made him feel like no other woman had ever made him feel before. He knew he had a lot of work to do to get himself together: a better paying job and a place, so they could have privacy underneath their own roof.

As they continued seeing each other, they began putting all their love and trust into each other, and their relationship got stronger and stronger. Brandy began seeing Chris a lot more, not just once or twice a week. It turned into four times a week. She wasn't trying to have him over every single day because she didn't want her sister to get tired of seeing him at her house. When he did come over, he would always bring over a bottle of wine. He never came empty handed. She would always find herself pre-warning him that all she needed was one glass. Like always, he looked at her and smiled saying, "Okay."

Brandy and her new boyfriend Chris sat at the kitchen table. Along with Chris bringing over the bottle, he also brought over

Chinese food. They wanted to eat something before they started drinking. Brandy learned her lesson at the last gathering she and her family had last year. She had not eaten anything, but she took her first sip. Thirty minutes later, she was slumped over the toilet with her head hanging as she sat on the floor. How embarrassing it was for her parents and her cousins to see her like that as they all stood in the doorway of the bathroom. Her dad had to get her off the floor and carry her to the bedroom because she couldn't walk. Never did she want to relive that drunken moment.

Sitting at the table laughing, eating and drinking in the middle of the day, Brandy and Chris were there alone. Before they knew it, they realized, like each and every time, they drank the whole bottle. Every time he would go to visit her, she seemed to wear those dresses he liked. The ones that gave him easy access to slide his hands up between her legs massaging her center part until it was steamy hot and moist.

She always like when he did that. It made her feel good and the feeling always made them lead right into sex. That made him become closer to her, and all he wanted to do was to continue to make her feel like he is all she needed. Whatever she needed, it didn't matter. All he wanted to do was be that man to handle it for her, from her cellphone bill to her credit card bill. He started paying them for her. And, Chris was spending a lot of money making sure Brandy went wherever she wanted him to take her.

No matter the restaurant or place they went to, they seemed to always have the best of fun. Their chemistry was great. It was if they had known each other longer than they actually did. They always tried to stay out as long as they could never wanting their night to end. When she went back home, she was quiet, always with her heels in her hand, trying not to awaken Katrina and Gary.

Because they would get to Katrina and Gary's about one or two in the morning most nights, Brandy always let Chris stay over and get some sleep. Most of the time, they would still be wired up, so they would spend a few hours just lying next to each other staring at each other as they talked before knocking out to sleep. Brandy always woke Chris up before seven o'clock to leave. She then hooked up with him in the afternoon.

Falling back into a deep sleep after Chris left, Gary always found his way into the bed with her still not waking her to see if she wanted to have sex. He just assumed. After she awakened from him going in and out of her with an early stiff one, he would pull out and just stare at her as he lay right beside her.

As she stared at him from the corner of her eye watching him, he would always begin to slowly rub his hands on her legs. Brandy could never pull herself to tell him to stop. His touch felt too good. In her own world, she felt liked he belonged to her. She felt stuck between two men. Brandy told him, "I see why my sister is so in love with your ass."

"I knew you couldn't resist it," he told her.

"Whatever, man," she said as they smiled.

Chapter 2
Before She Finds Out

Katrina was starting to get a little suspicious. She didn't really know what answers she was looking for, but she just had the feeling something was not right. She started thinking her husband had been acting a little differently lately, but she didn't know why. He stopped answering all her phone calls in the mornings before he made it to work, and he hadn't asked for sex lately. Even though she knew she wouldn't have sex with him on the three nights a week she worked overtime because she got home late and would be too tired, she still wondered why he hadn't asked.

Gary also seemed a little distant every night at dinner when the three of them were at the dinner table. Katrina noticed Brandy was acting a little differently too. Brandy was always tensed up like something was wrong, or she was acting uncomfortable about something. She just wasn't acting like her normal self. Katrina had been paying attention to her sister, but she just didn't know what was wrong with her lately. Katrina thought maybe she was putting more on the situation than she needed to.

Katrina tried to figure Brandy out without asking her directly. She wondered if maybe Chris was already acting stupid or driving Brandy crazy or something. When Chris would come over, Katrina could clearly see that was not the case.

The last thing Katrina would have thought of was her own husband as the one who had been driving Brandy crazy. Katrina did notice Brandy wouldn't act distant if it were just the two of them or even if Chris were there. Brandy only acted distant when Gary was in the room. Katrina noticed the changes in them both.

One morning, Katrina left the house with many things on her mind. That morning Brandy was home alone relaxing and watching T.V as she had been doing since she had been there for these past four months. Normally, she would at least try and have the house cleaned before her sister Katrina got home, by starting to clean in the morning. But that one day, she didn't start until the afternoon.

At noon, Brandy awoke from a nap. An hour later, she finally got off the couch to start to vacuum. As she bent over to turn on the vacuum to get the floor cleaned before she went to the other chores, she heard keys at the front door. She knew it wasn't Katrina because it was only 1:00 pm, and she was not off until 5pm that day. So, she figured it was Gary. As the door opened, she looked and saw it was Katrina. Standing very stiffly, Brandy saw a look in Katrina's eyes. She wasn't expecting her so early. The day when it was only Brandy alone in the house without company, Katrina had something to ask her.

By the look in Katrina's eyes, Brandy knew Katrina knew something or she wanted to know something. Brandy panicked. Brandy prayed her sister had not found out about her and Gary. As she nervously stood there, she felt any minute sweat was about to start dripping. As Katrina was positioning her lips to say the words she was about to say, Brandy's heart began pounding very quickly. It had to have been beating at least a thousand beats per minute. Standing nervously, instant sweat appeared on her forehead. She was hoping Katrina didn't notice the drops of sweat that began falling down that she quickly wiped away. She could barely move as she slowly calmed down by taking deep breaths.

"Brandy, you haven't done anything with Gary have you?" Katrina asked, as she stared with those suspicious eyes.

Brandy looked at her with a look of "Seriously!" With a straight face, Brandy said, "No, K! Why would you ask me something like that? I wouldn't do that to you. Chris is the only man I sleep with in my bed. He's my boo, and I'm feeling him. You are my sister, not my homegirl. I wouldn't even do that to any of my homegirls. Katrina, I would not sleep with your husband!"

Katrina said as she looked at Brandy, "I don't know why I asked you that. I'm sorry, sis. I'm tripping. I do apologize for asking that question." Nervously as she stood still, Brandy was hoping her sister couldn't see the guilt in her eyes. "Do you forgive me? I tripped out," Katrina said.

Brandy told her, "Oh, no. It's okay," as she bit her bottom lip nervously, from lying through her teeth. *Whew! Close call,* Brandy said to herself because she thought Katrina knew something.

While Brandy looked at Katrina saying it was okay, she was thinking, *Yeah right! I'm supposed to believe you're sorry. I know you think I'm sleeping with your husband.* Already knowing how crazy her sister can get, Brandy knew deep down Katrina didn't know anything because she would have been trying to fight her already.

Katrina's mind had been going crazy. She didn't know what the hell was going on. Lately, Gary had seemed a little preoccupied with his time. She just knew something was up. Brandy felt what she had just told Katrina was the best thing she could have told her. Brandy was thinking Katrina was home for the day early. After Katrina questioned Brandy, she left. Even though Brandy was in shock that her sister asked her that, after Katrina left, she went back to cleaning up the house. Later, Gary came home.

Hearing the door, Brandy didn't make any sudden gestures not knowing if they were about to walk in together. After the door shut and hearing only his voice besides hers in the house, Brandy quickly hopped off the couch looking behind her at him.

"What the hell do you think you're doing, Gary?" Brandy asked quickly as soon as Gary walked through the front door before her sister came home again. As she pulled him by the arm and into the kitchen, Gary had a crazy look, as he wondered what had gotten into Brandy. She told him, "Earlier, Katrina came home. She started asking me all types of questions thinking we are sleeping around."

Standing there, Gary looked shocked with an amused expression on his face and his mouth wide open. Gary looked at her waiting for an answer.

"So, what did you tell her?" Gary asked her.

"Duh!! I told her, 'Yeah, sis. I'm sleeping with your husband.' Crazy! Hello! I said, 'No,' and then I asked why she would ask me something like that, and then she said she was tripping and that she was sorry she asked me that question and that was it. And, I told her I would never do anything like that."

Gary then pulled Brandy close to his chest. Brandy tried to resist by pulling her arms away from him. As she still stood close to him, he pulled her even closer to his chest. He pulled her as close as he could, trying to force some tongue action upon her. Forcing his tongue into Brandy's mouth, he was trying to get a kiss in. She didn't resist for that long before she stopped to slowly open her mouth for him. They began kissing non-stop wrapping their arms around each other very tightly.

They could tell they missed each other. They headed for the living room to the couch. Pulling out her bed, they immediately hopped on, getting a quickie in before Katrina got off. Gary rolled Brandy over, so he could be on top. He began to stare into Brandy's eyes. Then, he began kissing her making his tongue go in deep. It was so good that he went in deeper and then deeper, just plunging it in. Gary was so into it that he didn't even hear the sound of the keys rambling at the door. But, Brandy heard it. She quickly pushed him off her with the sounds of a whisper saying to him with her eyes enlarged, "That's Katrina at the door!"

Gary quickly ran to the room quietly and hopped into the shower, damn near slipping inside almost busting his head. Brandy lay there and pretended to be asleep. Katrina walked in and didn't notice anything different. Brandy was still lying on the sofa bed, back in that same spot she was in this morning when Katrina had left for work. As Katrina walked by her she thought, *I bet she hasn't looked for a job.* But, she could tell by looking around Brandy had cleaned up. *At least, she did that,* Katrina thought.

Katrina had no idea how long Brandy was planning on staying in her home. She noticed Brandy would talk about getting a job and getting her own place, but all she saw was Brandy sleeping in the same spot every day on the couch. Brandy was her only sister and that was the reason she tolerated her.

"Hey, babe!! I'm home," she yelled out to Gary hoping he could hear her through the sounds of the shower water. She put her purse down on the kitchen counter; then, she went to the refrigerator to see if the meatloaf from two days ago was still inside. Yes, it was. She was so hungry and really didn't feel like cooking. She added some corn and made some cornbread to go with it. By the time Gary finished his shower, dinner was ready. It didn't take that long to cook because the main course was already done. Gary walked in and gave his wife a warm kiss and hug, letting her know how much he had missed her. She began telling him about her crazy day with one of her clients.

As Brandy continued to lay there still playing it off, she ended up falling asleep for real. On the other couch, Katrina and Gary sat eating the food she had just made while they watched T.V together. Katrina still knew nothing of the affair. When Brandy awoke, Katrina and Gary were still sitting on the couch watching a movie.

"Brandy, I left some food on the stove for you," Katrina said once she saw her waking up.

Brandy got up and took a shower, trying to get the sex smell off. She hoped Katrina couldn't smell her. After getting out the shower, she made her plate and watched a movie with them. Sitting there as Brandy ate her food, Katrina wanted to say something as she stared at her sister and her husband, but she didn't know how Brandy would take it. On the couch watching a movie together, Gary was having filthy thoughts of grabbing that big ass booty of Brandy's and fucking the shit out that ass. Deep in her heart, Brandy really felt bad for what had been happening, along with the feelings that had been growing between her and Gary.

Sitting and watching T.V, Gary and Katrina both seemed happy as they cuddled up together. Brandy was sitting there eating her food, but she was feeling very awkward and out of place sitting with them. Every chance Gary got, he made eye contact with her.

After the movie was over, Gary and Katrina called it a night and went to bed. Like always, Katrina fell asleep first. Once she had fallen into a deep sleep, with no hope of waking up any time soon, Gary gently reached over her to retrieve her cell. He looked through all her numbers of incoming and outgoing calls. After that, he clicked on the messages to look at her text messages. He spent an hour reading all her messages that had been on her phone for months.

Just in case she had been thinking about snooping around on him trying to catch him doing something he had no business doing, he downloaded a GPS into her phone, so wherever she went, he would know it. He would know where she was at all times without her even knowing he knew. He figured he would get to it before she thought of doing something like that to him. That way he would not get caught.

Gary gently put her phone back on her side of the bed on the dresser. After Gary finished watching the ten o'clock news, he turned off the TV and went to bed too.

The next day, Gary was trying to throw Katrina off, so he sent flowers to her job. When Katrina arrived back into the office and saw them sitting on her desk, they put a smile on her face.

After work, she couldn't wait to get home, so she could thank him in person. As soon as she walked in, he was already waiting for her with a bottle of wine. They gave each other a hug as their bodies pressed together.

"Babe, the flowers you sent today were beautiful."

"Oh, thank you," he told her.

Then, the two set the mood right and enjoyed the rest of their evening. For two weeks, Gary sent flowers. After the second week, Katrina began to wonder what was up with the flowers all of a sudden. Katrina wondered why he was sending her flowers every week to the office. It wasn't their anniversary or anything. She wondered if he was probably doing something wrong and using flowers to cover it up.

When she got home, she told him, "Baby, I love the flowers you sent last week and today."

He said, "I know, babe. That's why I sent them, because I know how much you love the smell of fresh roses, so I thought why not."

He was guilty for what he was doing, but not even him feeling guilty was going to make him stop. He couldn't stop getting what he wanted. After all, Brandy was giving him something his wife wasn't.

On week number three, he was still sending flowers. They were beautiful and all, but Katrina worried why he kept doing it. It was out of nowhere, and she wondered why. She appreciated it, but she hoped it wasn't a cover up for something bad he was doing.

He gave himself a few days before getting together again with Brandy. He called her up to have her to meet up with him at the Starbucks next to Panda Express. Brandy had her friend Ernie's car all day handling business. Using his car made it easy for her to meet up with Gary when he called. Once Brandy made it to the plaza, she realized she had not eaten yet, so while she waited for him to pull up, she grabbed something to eat from Panda. She sat in Ernie's car and ate, so when Gary pulled up, she could start the ignition and leave.

He pulled up moments later, and she closed up her food, started the car and followed behind him. They drove up to the drive-in. He paid for both of their cars to get in. They were not trying to actually watch the movie. They were just trying some place different each time they hooked up, so they didn't get caught up. But, Gary had to be careful being in public with her.

Once they had parked, she got out of the car and into his. She had parked right next to him. Entering his car, they kissed. "Let's get some food and snacks from the concession stand," Gary said.

"I'll get some snacks. I just had Chinese food while I was waiting for you."

"Okay," he told her. "Well, I need to eat. I haven't eaten anything all day."

Gary had got out the driver's side and went over to his passenger side to open the door for Brandy. The two walked to the concession stand holding hands. They returned with a bucket of popcorn, M & M's, Red Vines, and a medium size pepperoni pizza. Gary and Brandy both got back into the car getting in the back seat, as if they were going to actually watch the movie. Gary ate the whole box of pizza. Then, they ate a few handfuls of popcorn. At the same time, she was stuffing Red Vines in her mouth. Then, they sat the rest of the snacks on the floor.

Gary began lifting up her shirt to kiss her navel, while laying her back very slowly. Squeezing himself between her thighs in the back seat of his car, where they lay all cramped up with foggy windows, he teased her with his tongue. He flicked his tongue fast back and forth against her front center. Once again, they had the greatest time with each other.

During the middle of the week, just days later, he phoned Brandy on her cell to have her come up to his job. Brandy called

Ernie to see if she could borrow his car for the day again, but he needed it. So, she paid for a cab to meet up with Gary. She arrived to his workplace about 1:30 in the afternoon. Before having the cab driver pull into the parking area, she called him. That's when he instructed her to pull into the parking structure and go up to the rooftop. As she waited for him, he came walking up about five minutes later. Brandy thought he wanted to take a drive somewhere.

She figured that wasn't the case when he chirped his alarm on his car and pulled her along into the back seat with him. After getting in the back seat, his phone started going off just as he was about to turn it on silent. It was Katrina. He almost didn't answer it when he saw it was her, but he knew if he didn't she might try and make a trip to his job. Answering her call, she wanted to know if he forgot about meeting up for lunch. At the time, they would normally have lunch together every Thursday and Friday at the same time at the same restaurant.

Their weekly ritual of clearing all schedules and appointments to have their afternoon free to spend time together was broken. While Katrina couldn't wait to see her hubby, he was lying in the backseat of his car about to make love to her sister.

"Oh, shoot," he said.

"Baby, I totally forgot. I've been so tied up today," he said. Katrina asked him where he was, and he told her he was in a business meeting. Leaning back, Brandy was rubbing her hands all across his back. She licked her lips, getting ready and moistened for his.

Katrina said, "Oh that's fine, baby. Just call me after your meeting. Love you."

"Love you, too," he told her as he hung up the phone. Katrina was annoyed at his reason for not making it knowing that had been their Thursday and Friday lunch ritual for some years now. But, his attention was back on Brandy. Making love with their tongues first was always the greatest part of the foreplay. She wasn't new to what he wanted. She stroked him up and down. She already knew just what he needed. His eyes were closed tightly as he in no time burst into an explosion of passion. Through his tinted windows, he knew no one could see even if they tried. So, he didn't worry at all about having sex in the car.

Later that evening, Katrina went back to the office and talked to Suzy, the receptionist at the real estate agency she worked for. Suzy had been divorced for a year now. She had caught her husband cheating with a woman who was twenty years younger than she. Katrina had been noticing a change for a while in Gary, but she had no idea or clue if he was cheating on her. So, she talked to Suzy for a little advice.

Suzy had told her how she found out her ex-husband was cheating on her. First, she downloaded an app on her phone called the 'cheating boyfriend' app, and with that app she was able to receive a call to her phone from any number that called his phone, whether he had an incoming or outgoing call or text message.

Katrina thought it would be a good idea to see what was having

Gary act so differently lately. She wanted to see if anything he was doing was concerning another woman or not. Katrina downloaded the app. She played along as if she didn't already know he had been seeing and talking to someone else. She was not quite sure yet who the girl was, but as soon as she found out, she planned to beat both of their asses.

Months later, Gary and Brandy continued the same pattern of sleeping together between the time Katrina left for work and the time Gary left for work. Gary and Brandy always turned their time together into them making out. After a really long kiss, the feeling would always make each other feel like the pleasure was rushing through their bodies. Then came the lovemaking. By the time they would finish, their bodies would be drenched in sweat causing them to need a shower, so they would take one together. Then, the two would begin their day as normal.

The different telephone numbers that came in to Gary's phone could just be his clients seeing about their deal or looking for a house. Katrina was not trying to give herself away by calling any of the numbers that could just be one of his clients. On the first couple of days of using the app, she noticed a few calls coming in as restricted calls. She wondered if they all were just clients looking for help with their credit or those who wanted to buy a home.

The text messages were a little different. Every text he received, the conversation appeared on Katrina's phone. Being the nice gentleman that he was, Gary approached any woman in conversation with 'dear heart' or 'baby,' so it was hard to tell with whom if anything more than business was taking place. Through her busy schedule with her booked up clients, she was only able to make it to some of the locations throughout the week where Gary was supposed to meet with some of these people. Only the woman whose calls weren't about business was the one she was focused on.

What Katrina found so crazy was by the time she would go to the location listed in the text, she would get there early just to see him sitting by himself reading a newspaper, looking as though he may be waiting for someone. But once he received a call, he would just leave. She would never see the person he was supposed to have met. Weeks of the same thing went by, and she still had not seen him with another woman. She was not sure why he was texting someone or someone was texting him to meet up with him when he was not meeting with anyone.

Through Gary's GPS locator, he knew where his wife was going all the time, so he started noticing every time he was supposed to have been meeting up with her sister, she was always popping up. Not once did he see her, but with the locator, he knew she was near. He continued to play it off because he didn't want her to figure anything out.

When Katrina would show up, Gary called Brandy to tell her not to come, at the last minute. Gary was on to his wife catching on to him. He was afraid his little fun was coming to an end. Back at the house, Gary would continue to tell Brandy, "I think she is on to us."

Still, Katrina hadn't said anything to Brandy. Katrina didn't really know anything yet, so she was still trying to find out. Something just didn't seem right. Katrina was not going to give up. It was her intuition, and she was going to keep digging until she got the information she was looking for. She couldn't believe she was even thinking the thoughts she had.

That was the first time during their marriage that she had those types of feelings about her husband, and she knew once the feelings were there, the assumption was usually right. So, she needed to talk to him face to face.

On her drive home, she got caught in the Friday evening traffic. Everyone was getting off work trying to get somewhere through the crazy 405 traffic. Katrina was thinking while sitting in traffic that it had been truly a crazy couple of weeks for her.

Once she got home, she couldn't wait to kick off her shoes. She had had a long day at work and had waited all day to talk to her husband. She needed clarity; she needed answers. She didn't want to get straight into what she wanted to talk to him about, so she waited until after dinner.

After dinner and after they had taken a shower, she started the conversation. He hoped like hell she still didn't know. He planned to say whatever he had to say to take away all her worries about him doing anything against her. They talked all night long, until they both were ready to fall asleep. He held her arms close, bringing her closer to him.

"Look into my eyes," he told her. "I love you, and I would never do anything to hurt you. I promise."

She kissed him. "I love you so much, baby. I'm sorry for thinking that crazy shit." Then, the two went to sleep.

During the early morning, she felt his hardness tap her thigh. Their lips drew in closer, and they kissed slowly. As he kept pushing his tongue in deeper, he slid inside consuming her. She arched into him with every thrust he made. Gary began tracing his tongue on her breasts. She started moaning, with her eyes closed shut as he continued.

After a while, they rolled over. She ended up on top. She felt the firmness of his hands gripping her butt as he massaged it. Shortly afterward, he asked her to sit up on it. He sat up a little still gripping firmly onto her butt as he moved her back and forth on him. The moans got louder. She was gliding back and forth on it. She felt all of him inside her. It felt like it was in her stomach. Katrina grabbed his neck, and they wrapped their arms around each other. The speed changed, and they began going faster until they both exploded.

The next day, she thought about going to Vegas for the weekend to relieve some stress. When she made it home from work, she talked to Gary about going to Vegas. It had been a while since they had been. He agreed, so they decided to go away to Las Vegas for the weekend. They quickly packed a bag, and they were ready to go. They then tried to figure out if they wanted to make it a couples' thing and invite their friends, or if it was just going to be the two of them. They decided that it was just going to be them.

Gary wanted to blow off some money but hoped to come back home with way more than he left with. Katrina was trying to win some money. The last time she went, she lost all the money she went with. She was surely not doing that again. The most she planned to lose was forty dollars. Halfway there, Gary decided to keep driving all the way there after looking over at Katrina for the past hour and seeing her laid back in the passenger seat getting some sleep in. She look liked she needed it. At least he knew after getting some rest, she was not going to have a problem staying up all night with him.

Right when he was about to see the sign that says welcome to Las Vegas, Gary began waking her up. Katrina woke up and started yelling out the window. "Yeah, we're in Vegas, baby!!"

After getting into Vegas, they stopped at the casino they were going to be staying at first. They wanted to play a few games before going to check in; they were feeling lucky.

As soon as Gary and Katrina sat down at the slot machines, out of nowhere a waitress with blonde hair popped up to bring over a tray of drinks. Trying to go from one slot machine to the next with their luggage was a tad bit difficult.

It would have been easier if they would have checked-in and taken their bags to their rooms first. Eventually, they did just that. Then, they went back to the casino and had more drinks. Katrina played the slots, while Gary also played slots, but he was on the black jack table more.

Later, they left Caesar's Palace to walk the strip. They had not been in their room for literally more than a minute since they had been in Vegas. Later, when they did get back to the room, they were drunk and happy for some reason. They were on a little vacation, and the two were having fun gambling and enjoying themselves. Earlier, she was bringing him luck; as long as she stood there, he kept winning. Now back at the room in the early morning, she went to use the bathroom before they were about to take a quick shower together.

When Katrina went to use the bathroom, she noticed drops of blood falling into the water. After she wiped herself with more tissue, she looked, and there was more blood coming out than what appeared on the tissue she was holding between her legs. *Damn, out of all nights to start my period why tonight? Why this weekend?* she wondered. Her being on her period or her starting her period really wasn't going to matter to him. They knew how to work around that.

They went and got into the shower. He immediately brought his head closer to her chest; then, he began sucking her breasts. She then tried to reach down and stroked his penis while he was sucking on her breasts, but she was unable to reach it. So, she started sucking on his ears and kissing all over his forehead. Then, they both began feeling a sensation rush through their bodies and that's where they stayed to have passionate sex.

Gary gripped her around her waist, picking her up off the floor of the tub, and rested her on his hips as he went in. Katrina also had a grip around his neck, so she wouldn't fall. When Gary couldn't stand in that position anymore, he then stood behind her gripping her hips taking it in nice and slowly as he watched the water roll down her back.

After they both had cum, she turned around looking at him giving him a smile. He grabbed a face towel from the shower rod and placed a lot of soap on it. Then, he began scrubbing her body. After he was done with her body, he passed the towel to her and then she scrubbed his body with the same towel. After they were done in the shower, they dried off and kissed. She put on a pair of panties, and he put on a pair of boxers. Then, they both went to bed and knocked out. The two were drained of their energy.

Once they woke up, she went to use the bathroom. When she was finished, she washed her hands. After she looked up and glanced in the mirror, she saw her unruly, wild hair. They had a lot of fun last night in that shower.

After they got up, Katrina combed her hair, and they both got dressed. Then, they went to eat at a buffet and back to the casino they went. Afterwards, they walked the strip for a few hours. They shopped at some stores later that evening before going back to the room. They were both ready for another romantic night.

That night when they got back to the room, they took a shower together. When they were done and dried off, she put a tampon on, and they both remained naked and headed for the bed.

Getting onto the bed, slowly he lowered her head down as he lay back. She wrapped her hands around it and began sucking on it. She had all types of ways to pleasure her husband. Her period wasn't stopping anything. To the early morning, they were doing all types of crazy freaky stuff. They didn't go to sleep until three in the morning, and they didn't awaken until noon. They were still tired, and when they woke up, they woke up sluggish and moved around the room slowly.

On their last night there, Gary wanted to take her to see Absinthe in the white tent. After hearing about the show and how cool it was from a couple of random people at the casino, he wanted them to check it out. The tickets were only $99 per ticket, so after paying for two, they went and got dressed and made it to the eight o'clock show because the ten o'clock show would have been too late.

After leaving the show when it was over, they went right next to the tent to a restaurant and ordered the Las Vegas Strip Steak Sandwich. It was so good and very fulfilling. Katrina really couldn't eat anymore after eating that, but Gary wanted to order an apple cobbler that he ended up making her take a few bites of. They went back to the room to turn in for the night. As they left out that next morning to go back home, Katrina kissed Gary, letting him know that was the type of fun that was due for the both of them.

"I'm telling you, Katrina. That is what we needed."

"Yes, I do agree."

"Now when we get home, it's back to making some money," he said.

Chapter 3

Brandy's Delivery Room Moment

Brandy wanted to move out the house before Katrina found out she had been sleeping with her husband. Brandy was getting tired of living a lie while loving both Gary and Chris. That was not supposed to even be possible. She hadn't told anyone yet that she had missed her period. She was already two weeks late. She found herself going over to the 99-cent store to pick up a pregnancy test. After taking it, it showed a positive result. *No,* she thought. *Maybe it's not accurate coming from the 99-cent store.*

An hour later, she went to the drug store to buy another pregnancy test. Brandy was in the bathroom staring at two pregnancy tests, not one test, but now two. Standing there mad at herself for letting something like that happen when she knew better.

Both tests showed two dark straight lines: a positive test result. Pregnant. Yes, she was that for sure. That's what she had wondered when she had realized she was late. Too much of that good morning sex with the man she had no business having sex with at all. She thought about putting it back inside the brown paper bag and tossing it in the trash can outside, but she ended up keeping it and tossing it inside her purse to show Gary the two lines on the stick.

Before leaving the bathroom, she looked around one more time to make sure she didn't leave anything in there she shouldn't be leaving. Afterward, she left the house. She couldn't even imagine what Gary was going to say once she told him. She always wanted a good man to have a family with but not like this. Definitely not like this at all. Because she was still not convinced of the test results, she made her a doctor appointment for the next day to see her gynecologist for confirmation.

The next day, she went to the doctor, only to find out she really was pregnant. *Damn, shit just got real,* she thought to herself. Leaving the doctor's office, she didn't even want to go home to her sister's right away.

Deciding to keep her first baby, she knew once her sister or anyone in their family found out, they would all be disappointed with her. They may even stop talking to her too, but she knew she was not getting rid of her baby. She was just going to have to deal with the consequences later. Brandy didn't want to face anyone; she didn't want to see Chris, nor Gary's ass and definitely not Katrina. She was facing a very big problem.

She walked over to her friend Ernie's house. He didn't live too far from where she was at the moment. She wanted to chill over there and talk to him while she gathered her thoughts. When she made it there, all she wanted to do was curl up on his couch and cry. Upon her entry, he gave her a hug. She didn't seem like herself, so he knew she was going through something and she needed a hug.

"Aww, friend. Is everything okay?" he asked.

She cried, "No."

"What's going on? Is there something I can do to help?"

"No, I think I did enough," she said sadly. "Oh, wait! Hold up. There is one thing you can do."

"Name it! And it's done."

"You can let me stay here with you for a week."

"K put you out?" his eyes widened.

Brandy looked at him while she hesitated to answer the question.

"Tell me what's going on. I'm here to help."

"No, but if she finds out I'm pregnant by her husband, she will kill me," Brandy told him.

That was not the answer Ernie was expecting to hear. "Girl, clearly that is a bad joke. Stop playing. For real, what's going on?" He looked serious while he thought she was joking around. She shook her head slowly and told him it was not a joke. Ernie was almost likely to pass out from hearing that.

When what she just told him finally registered in his head, he told her of course she could stay for a week.

"Thank you, Ernie for real," she said to him with a worried look in her eye.

"So, bitch!! What are you going to do?" he asked with concern.

"I don't even know yet," she told him.

Later that evening, Brandy dialed Gary's phone at a time she knew Katrina shouldn't have been home yet. Gary felt a vibration in his pocket. He pulled his cell out and saw it was Brandy. He didn't want to answer because Katrina was home early and just a few steps away inside the shower. However, he quickly answered and quietly told Brandy he was going to have to talk to her when she came home after Katrina was asleep.

"Damn! She's already there?" she whispered to him.

"Yeah, she's in the shower," he told her.

"Well, Gary, I wasn't coming home tonight," she told him. "And what I have to say can't wait."

Gary asked with a concerned tone, "What can't wait? Is everything okay, Brandy?"

She said, "Gary, I'm pregnant." Through the silence after she said that she asked, "Gary, did you hear me?"

Once Brandy began to hear Katrina in the background asking who he was on the phone with, before he could respond with, "Yeah," she immediately hung up the phone. That left him in shock mode, thinking to himself how he would tell his beautiful wife of seven years that he was having an affair with her sister and got her pregnant. Just a year before this, he could have never seen himself being the unfaithful type of husband. Now, the pressure was on stronger now that Brandy was pregnant.

Days went by, and she hadn't been to the house. Katrina and Gary both wondered were Brandy had been spending her nights for the past few days. At first, they assumed she had been at Chris' house until he called that day looking for her.

When Brandy left Ernie's house, she left with a clear head. Her stopping by and him letting her stay that week helped. She needed that talk and the time to just think and get her mind together. That morning, she went out on a hunt for a job. When she finally did go back home to her sister's, it was a relief for Katrina. She was really worried about her sister.

Brandy started getting up every morning trying to find a job. Katrina and Gary both saw her less. After a month went by of putting in applications every single day, she still had not received a phone call for an interview.

Two more weeks went by and Brandy still hadn't found a job yet. She was still trying to stay gone more, for she was ashamed to face her sister. Time was still passing, and Brandy had plans to ask Gary to help her because he was the reason she was in the situation she was in. Feeling bad for what she had been doing was too late now, as she was two and a half months pregnant with his baby.

Ever since the day she found out she was pregnant, it had been awkward for her to be around anyone, so she had to leave. She felt really horrible right then for the shit she and Gary had done that led up to all of that. Damn, she didn't know what else to do besides leave.

Packing up all her things, she never thought she would be moving out due to a reason such as that one. After packing up all her things and whatever else she had accumulated in the whole year she had been there, she scrolled through her cell looking for her homegirl Jordan's number. She almost didn't want to call her because it had been about a month since she last spoke to her, and she didn't want it to seem like she was only calling because she needed something, but shit she really needed a ride to go look for an apartment.

After finding Jordan's number, Brandy called her. The phone rang, but the call ended up going straight to voicemail. Brandy looked down at the phone, thinking, *Wow, I can't believe what just happened.* So, Brandy tried scrolling through her phone again to Misty's number. Neither of them talked often, but they were so cool that never mattered. They always looked out for each other. But, she had no luck with calling Misty; her number had changed. Brandy wasn't on Facebook regularly, but she went on it to go to Misty's page, to send her a message. Seconds later, Brandy had an incoming call, and it was her girl Jordan.

"Hello?"

"Hey, girl. Sorry about that. Right when I tried to answer your call, my phone died."

"Oh, no worries. But, I was wondering if you're not busy right now if you felt like taking me to go see about an apartment."

"Oh, no. I'm not doing anything. Where are you?"

"At my sister's."

"Alright. I will be over there in a minute."

Once Jordan arrived, Brandy was happy to see her friend. She had all her things sitting on the porch. She knew she wasn't going back. She was determined to find her something that day. Brandy ended up liking the first apartment they stopped at called the Sunset

Manor Apartments. It wasn't even too far from her parents' house. Brandy was looking for a studio or a one bedroom. She was given a tour inside one of the apartments, and she really liked it.

"I like it. Do you have any studios or one bedrooms ready?" she asked.

"How soon are you looking to move in?"

"Today."

"Well, I will have a studio and two one bedrooms at the beginning of the month, but that's three weeks away."

Brandy couldn't wait that long; she needed something right then. "Okay well, what do you have ready right now that I can move into right now?" Brandy asked.

"I have a two bedroom available right now."

She really didn't want anything that big; it was only her. She had already let her ride leave, and she had all her bags. So, she decided to take it anyway. Because it was Brandy's first time getting an apartment, they used her sister's home as a place of reference, even though she wasn't paying any rent there. But, she told them she did. After completing the application, she was done. All she needed was $500 for the deposit. The only person who came to mind was Gary. Brandy called Gary at work. She didn't bother calling his cell. As soon as he got on the phone, she got straight to the point of why she was calling him.

"Gary, I need $500 for a deposit for an apartment."

He was surprised to hear her voice. He hadn't really spoken to her lately; she had been gone every time he looked up. Before he answered her question, he asked if she was keeping the baby or not.

"Yes, I'm keeping the baby. Why do you think I'm moving out before my sister finds out anything?"

He was quiet for a second.

"Where are you right now? At the house?" he asked her.

"No, I'm at the Sunset Manor Apartments."

"That's not too far from your mom's, right?"

"Yes, so how soon can you get here?"

"I can be there in about two hours."

"Okay, but first let me see if they can take payment over the phone because I have all my stuff down there sitting in the office. I need to move in now."

"Okay."

"Okay, I'll call you back."

"Brandy!!" he shouted, trying to catch her before she hung up the phone.

"Yeah?"

"Look, the only way I will help you and the baby is if you will keep all this a secret. Your sister can never find out. Nobody can."

"I know."

They both hung up the phone. Brandy had a little power to control him because all she had to do was blackmail him by saying, "If you don't help with my apartment, I will tell Katrina what you did." Luckily, she didn't have to say that, but if he would have had a different response, that's what she would have said. She didn't know what the hell he was thinking anyway; she planned to take their secret to the grave.

There was not a thought about whether or not she was going to keep the baby. Even though her pregnancy was unplanned and very much unexpected, she was just going to keep who she was pregnant by a secret, for her sake, her baby's sake, and for Gary's sake. He didn't want Brandy telling anyone, and she agreed. Brandy wasn't planning on saying a word to anyone. However, there had been a lot of times when she felt the need or the want to tell her sister or even her homegirl Jordan or even Misty, but she just never did.

After hanging up the phone, Brandy went to ask the apartment manager about taking payments over the phone, but she said the deposit had to be in the form of a check or a money order. Brandy didn't want to hear that because that meant she had to wait those two hours she didn't want to wait for.

Brandy had to hang out in the lobby while waiting for Gary to get off work. Brandy sat there thinking about calling Chris. He didn't even know about her being pregnant yet. She made her mind up to call him after she got into the apartment.

She already knew people were probably going to assume it was Chris', and once they did, she wasn't going to say any differently. Brandy was never woman enough to tell her sister the truth. She never wanted to be the reason Katrina's heart was crushed.

Gary showed up as soon as he got off work. He paid the deposit for her apartment, and he even paid her rent for three months. She wasn't going to have to worry about paying rent for four months, as her first month was going to be free. Brandy was so very happy. She thanked him with a long kiss and hug. Gary took all her things for her up to her apartment. He didn't stay. After he took her things up for her, he also left her three hundred dollars as well. After all that, she knew it was going to be pretty easy to get just about anything she asked from him.

When Brandy moved out earlier that day, she had promised herself she wasn't going to have sex with him anymore. She didn't tell him that; that's just what she told herself. Once she settled in, Brandy contacted Chris to tell him about the apartment; he was excited for her. She gave him the address, and he came over. While he was on his way, she tried to figure out how she would tell him she was pregnant.

When Katrina got home later that day, Brandy and all her things were nowhere in sight. Katrina made a quick call to Brandy. She wanted to ask her, "Why the sudden move?" Brandy saw her sister's call coming in on her cell.

"Hello?" she answered.

"Hey, Brandy."

"Hey, K. What's up?"

"Umm, that's what I wanted to know. Is everything okay? I see you have moved out."

"Oh, no. Everything is fine," she kind of giggled a little, so she could sound believable to Katrina.

"Are you sure?"

"Yeah, K."

"Okay, Brandy"

"It was just about that time, sis, to get my own place."

"Okay, now you know you can always come back."

"Thank you for letting me know that, but thank you for everything you've done by helping me out for all the time that you did."

Katrina was a little bit happy about her sister's sudden move, but she wasn't going to tell her that. All Brandy had done was lay around and damn near sleep all damn day anyway. She had not even tried to better her situation by looking for a job. Katrina couldn't blame Brandy for her laziness when their parents had babied her for her whole life. Her ass didn't know any better.

"Well, Brandy, you know girl, I'm just a phone call away if you need anything."

"I know," Brandy said.

Katrina almost wanted to ask her sister how she got an apartment with no job, but she didn't want to get too much in Brandy's business. If she did, Brandy might start asking her for money, so Katrina just left that alone. She felt she should just be happy for her sister's accomplishment. She hung up the phone and cut the radio on. As soon as the song sounded, she began singing the song and snapping her fingers throughout the house. She felt good, so she cracked open two of her living room windows to allow some fresh outside air to come inside. She began swinging her long hair back and forth while singing to different songs and hitting every high note she thought she could hit. Although she was kind of off note, it didn't matter. She was there alone, and she felt damn good.

When Gary made it home, Katrina had the brightest smile on her face; she was filled with happiness and joy.

"Hey, baby," Katrina greeted him, with a kiss on his lips.

"Hey, baby," he said as he kissed and hugged her back.

"Babe, you know my sister moved out?"

"Oh, for real? Is everything okay? Where did she move?" he asked acting like he didn't already know.

"You know what? I didn't even ask. I guess I was more shocked that she even moved out and got her own place with no damn job." *That's crazy*, she thought. "You know this is cause for a drink," she told him. He stood there looking at her. She headed to the kitchen and pulled down two glasses from the cabinet.

"Oh, baby you're wrong."

"About what?" she asked him.

"You're happy she moved out."

"Yeah, I am, but I'm happier she found independence and finally got her own place for the first time. I'm happy about that."

Gary grabbed and poured the drink into their glasses.

"Let's make a toast."

"What are we toasting?" he asked.

"We're toasting to love, life, happiness, us and Brandy's independence."

He nodded his head in agreement to what she just said and then the two drank up. As they both sat at the dining room table drinking, they continued listening to the music on the radio. They both were getting pretty tipsy the more they drank.

"Ohhhh, that's my song right there," Katrina shouted.

Katrina got herself up from the chair and started dancing. She pulled Gary up right behind her. He held onto her waist, as she was moving her hips back and forth. He pulled her butt closer to his body, as she was grinding her body against him. They both danced with their drinks still in their hands.

After an hour or two, they had to convince themselves that they were not young in age anymore. They were out of breath and tired and knew they both needed to sit their asses down somewhere. They were partying, but it came to an end. They both went to go lay in the bed and watch television. They watched it until it began to watch them.

Meanwhile, Chris made it over to Brandy's. He liked the apartment, but what he liked the most was the person standing behind the door who had just let him in and was standing there with just a bra and panties on. That was Chris' first time seeing her in a week. He thought he had done something wrong and that was why he had not talked to her. They walked up to each other, pulling one another closely as they hugged and gave each other a wet kiss on the lips. After they hugged and kissed, Brandy looked at Chris very nervously.

"I'm pregnant." That's all she could say.

He was a kid all over again, jumping up and down with much excitement to be having his first child. What he didn't know was that it wasn't his baby. She looked at him seeing his joy that she didn't want to kill. She wondered if she told him that he was not the father what exactly would he do or what he would say. He probably would leave her. So, she decided not to tell him anything. She didn't want to be stuck taking care of a baby by herself.

Gary planned to give it two weeks before contacting Brandy; he wanted her to get settled in her apartment first, before trying to pop up over there to get some. He figured since he had to help her, she would still give him some pleasure in bed. He was starting to feel a little horny. So after two weeks, he thought he would give her a call. But when he called her asking if he could come over, she straight out said, "No! Gary, I'm not dealing with you like that anymore."

Gary said, "Brandy, I miss you. And, I still have the same feelings for you. Nothing has changed, just the fact you're in your own place now." Brandy admitted to him she missed him too. Gary wanted to still have sex from time to time, but Brandy refused and wasn't going for it anymore.

"Why not?" he asked her.

"That is just going to interfere with Chris and me. Gary, I do love Chris too. I'm in love with him, and I'm really trying to be serious with him, but it's so hard because I have you too."

Gary became upset with her.

"Let's just pretend this never happened," Brandy suggested.

"Brandy, how are we going to pretend? So, what are you saying? You're not fucking with me anymore?"

"It's like you are reading my mind."

"What are you saying?" he asked.

"I'm not fucking you anymore."

"So, you have no intention of fucking me anymore?"

She paused. "No, I don't," she sounded. "Bye, Gary. I have to go," and then, she hung up.

He didn't think that would be the end for Brandy. However, Brandy had learned a lot more about Chris from what makes him happy, upset, to his favorite food and snacks, his favorite color, and the music he likes. He also knew the same about her. The two remained happy together, and that was how she wanted to keep it. On the other hand, Gary had been having way too much fun with Brandy. He didn't know how to accept her "No" right then.

That wasn't what Gary was expecting to hear after finding out just weeks ago she was pregnant with his baby, and he had just put her in her own apartment. Gary mumbled to himself, *Maybe this was not a good time to call.* He decided to give her two more weeks.

Two weeks later, Brandy started calling Gary and bugging him about money. Even though he knew she wasn't dealing with him like that, he just went on and sent her some money. Gary was considering it to be hush money. Although Brandy didn't want to deal with Gary anymore, she still accepted his money. He paid her rent and made sure she kept money in her pocket.

Gary went back to being unhappy. He had enjoyed sex more than three times a week, sometimes every single day, and even twice in one morning. Katrina was still taking her work seriously, which was all she knew how to do, and she didn't notice her husband being unhappy.

One morning waking up feeling nauseous, Katrina didn't feel like getting out the bed. She knew for her that wasn't normal at all. She ended up calling her doctor. She knew something was wrong, and she really didn't want to take any pills to get rid of any sickness she had or for the way she was feeling. She was never a pill taker. Aloud she said, "I know I'm not pregnant." Gary turned around and looked at her with a look on his face that said, "Oh, damn!"

"Sweetie, maybe you should at least see a doctor just to see what he says," he said. He had spent the last two months trying to process the fact that Brandy was pregnant. The more he pretended not to have heard that, the more reality had sat in. Unfortunately, trying to forget was not working. Somehow, Katrina made it out the bed and went to her doctor's office to pay Dr. Miller a visit. Katrina knew Dr. Miller would also be happy to see her. It had been six months since she saw him last. When she arrived, she checked in at the front desk and waited until her name was called.

After sitting there for forty minutes, her name was then called. She went to the back with the nurse where they handed her a cup to urinate into. Afterwards, she gave the cup to the nurse. Then, she was instructed to have a seat in Room Two. She sat very nervously, as she waited for the results. After five minutes, the nurse came back and told her that her lines came out light.

She asked, "So what does that mean?"

"Well, that just means it's still too early to say, and because it did show two lines it's giving you a positive test result. But because it was so light, we have to wait a few more weeks to retest."

They scheduled her another appointment for three weeks from that day. When her appointment date came up, Katrina was ready to see her doctor. As soon as she stepped foot out the house, she became sick. She believed it was from the heat. That morning when Katrina watched the forecast, she saw it was going to be hot and sunny, but she didn't know it was going to be that hot. Her period still had not come yet. Right then, Katrina already knew what her results were going to be. As soon as she checked in, they were already ready for her to go to the back.

"Hey, how are you, Mr. and Mrs. Garrett?"

"I'm fine, Dr. Miller," she smiled.

"Fine," Gary said almost in a whisper.

"Well, that's good."

As Dr. Miller looked down at the nurse's notes, he looked up and stated, "Looks like what brings you in today is that you're feeling nauseous, sick, and weak, and that you believe you may be pregnant."

"Yeah, doctor. I have been feeling a bit strange. I just have not had any energy at all for almost a month now."

"Mrs. Garrett, when was your last period?"

"I really don't remember," she thought. "Well, I don't remember the exact date, but it's been about a month ago now."

"Well, did you have one this month?" She squinted her eyes

trying to remember. Katrina suddenly shook her head telling the doctor that she didn't think so.

He gave her a cup to urinate in, so she could take a pregnancy test. Ten minutes later, the doctor came back into her room and said, "Congratulations, Mrs. Garrett. You're pregnant." Katrina was so excited after all the years of trying. Hearing the good news, she couldn't wait for the baby to be born. Gary sat beside her still in shock. The doctor glanced over at Gary with a smile. He told him congratulations on their new baby. All you heard was silence before Gary told the doctor thank you.

Leaving the doctor's office, Katrina felt like a whole new person. Gary went to work, while she went home and rested. Later, she thought about her plate becoming fuller with her still working and having to keep up with doctor's appointments and the future classes she was going to have to remember to go to. Finding out earlier that day she was pregnant, she didn't know whether it was a mind thing or if she actually became sicker. That made things that much harder for her to make it through the night.

Katrina being sick as she was didn't make it any easier for Gary, with going back and forth to the store getting snacks or food to satisfy her cravings. Whether he liked it or not, he did everything his wife required. Because he had to continue to get up throughout the night, he couldn't go back to sleep. So, he got back out of bed and started working out on the bedroom floor, doing push-ups, sit ups, and jogging in place. Katrina still couldn't sleep either, feeling uncomfortable, so she stayed up watching TV and watching him at the same time. Between Katrina and Brandy, the two of them were driving him crazy.

Things are getting too carried away, Gary thought. Brandy had begun calling him, asking for money for designer bags and clothes. He was hoping like hell she wasn't only buying designer bags and clothes. He was hoping she was saving most of the money for the baby to buy the things their baby would need. He already knew Brandy was only using him for his money, because she wasn't trying to have sex anymore. He never said anything, because he knew as long as he kept doing what he was doing by sending her money every month, their secret would stay a secret.

Nearly four months pregnant, Brandy couldn't hide her popped out belly anymore, so she knew she couldn't continue to keep her pregnancy a secret.

"I feel sick. My stomach hurts," she told Chris.

"Well, what did you have to eat?"

"A boiled egg and some toast this morning."

"You haven't eaten lunch. You need to eat something. Don't forget, baby. You're eating for two." Chris went into the kitchen to prepare a meal for the two of them. Brandy leaned back onto the couch while he was in the kitchen cooking.

"So, have you told anyone in your family yet?"

"No."

His eyes widened. "Not even Katrina your own sister?"

"No, not yet. I was thinking about calling my mother to tell her."

"When was the last time you talked to her?"

"It's been a long while."

Her heart was pounding; she was scared to tell her mother because she knew she was going to ask a thousand questions. Nevertheless, Brandy ended up calling her mother to tell her she was going to have a grandchild in five months. She could hear her dad in the background saying, "She got pregnant that quick?"

"Stop it, Ricky," her mother told her husband.

"Katrina first, now you? Yeah right! It is not April Fool's Day, Brandy," she said.

When Brandy shared the news with her mother, she didn't believe her one bit because that was the second call she had received that day. The first one was from her sister Katrina. Their mother had no idea both her daughters would call her on the same day just hours apart saying the exact same thing.

"What! For real, Mom. I am! I'm not joking. I'm serious," Brandy insisted. Then she asked, "Mom, did you just say Katrina called saying the same thing too?"

"Yeah," she said. "She just found out this morning that she's six weeks pregnant."

Brandy said, "Wooowww!" She sat shaking her head from side to side telling herself, *How could I?* Her mother talked as she held her forehead in the palm of her hand. All she could think about was she had a bigger problem now with her and her sister both being pregnant by her sister's husband. Her mother then told her congratulations, and Brandy could hear the smiles through her mother's voice. She could tell her mother was happy about hearing her news. Once they got off the phone, Ricky asked his wife if Brandy told her who the father of her baby is.

"Well, honey I didn't ask."

"She probably doesn't know."

Ricky was disgusted with his daughter's choices. Eventually, Brandy knew her pregnancy would need to be explained. But until that day came, she wasn't going to say shit about it and would focus on getting her shit together before her baby was born.

Chris quickly made Brandy a bacon cheeseburger and fries. When he handed her the plate of food, he also handed her a box. She slowly took both with a smile. She, of course, sat the plate down first and opened the box. He got down on one knee and proposed to her with the ring that was in the box. He asked her if she would marry him, and she said yes. Brandy and Chris set the date for three years from that day.

Meanwhile, her mother Deborah called Katrina to tell her about Brandy being pregnant too.

"Hey, Ma," Katrina answered.

"Girl, you wouldn't believe what your sister just called and told me."

"What, Ma?"

"She just told me she is pregnant."

"Oh, for real!!" With excitement, Katrina screamed out on the phone.

"How far along is she?" she asked.

"She's four months," Deborah said.

After Katrina was done talking with her mother, she couldn't believe Brandy hadn't called her yet to tell her about her baby news. She wondered why it took her sister four months to say something about her pregnancy. Katrina was excited about her first little niece or nephew and knowing her baby would have a cousin the same age.

Katrina was smiling from ear to ear as if she was the one having Brandy's baby for her. Katrina couldn't wait to call Brandy. Katrina called up Brandy to tell her congratulations on her and Chris's new baby and about her baby news too.

Brandy paused and said, "Thank you." Then, she told her sister how happy she was about her news too. "But Katrina, that's not all. Chris just proposed to me," Brandy told her. Katrina was so happy for her sister.

After that day, Katrina often called up Brandy to invite her out to lunch in the middle of the day between her meetings with her clients. The two enjoyed their sisterly time together. They went out shopping for baby clothes every week, and later in their pregnancy, they both found out they were pregnant with girls.

Brandy decided she wanted a brighter future for her and her child. She didn't want to always be the needy one. Her sister was and had always been a big help to her, but she wanted to become self-sufficient. Seeing her sister and everything she had and had accomplished, Brandy wanted the same good life. So, she checked into a trade school to be a medical assistant, so she could be done around the time she had her daughter, or at least a little afterward. Getting her own place, finally being on her own, and being pregnant, Katrina saw that had forced Brandy to grow up.

Brandy was determined to get to school, so she caught the bus every day, making it there on time. She never missed a day. She studied hard every day to ace her modules. Chris was already going to school. He was into working on motorcycles, rebuilding them, and fixing them. But Chris would have only a little money after helping Brandy with her rent.

Whenever she was short for either bills or food, Katrina would come through for them. She never mind helping, as long as they were trying to do better for themselves. Some days, Katrina left work at her lunch break to stop at the grocery store to pick up food, fruit and snacks for herself and for her sister. When she got off work, she would take the groceries to her sister. Eating healthy was expensive, but it was what Katrina forced on herself and on her sister to ensure their babies would be born healthy. Reading pregnancy and parenting books to become the best mother for her unborn child was something else Katrina had taken on. She was a proud wife and mother to be. As time continued to go on, just like most expectant mothers, she couldn't wait.

One day when Katrina got off work, she began heading over to Brandy's apartment. When Katrina arrived, she found a parking spot right in front of the building. She walked up to Brandy's door, and after a few knocks on the door, Brandy answered.

"Hey, sis," she said as she entered Brandy's place. As Brandy opened the door all the way to let her sister in, Katrina kissed Brandy on her cheek and started rubbing her little round belly. Days ago, Brandy made seven months pregnant; Katrina was so excited about having a niece, so her daughter wouldn't have to be by herself. *My child will have a cousin to play with,* she thought.

"I have to apologize for the mess," Brandy said as Katrina walked inside looking at the clothes all over the living room and dishes all on the counter instead of being washed and put away. The mess disturbed Katrina to see her sister's messy place. She knew they didn't grow up like that.

Katrina only stayed for an hour visiting Brandy before going home to prepare dinner for Gary.

"Alrighty, sis. You take care of yourself. Remember, if you need anything, just holler. Love you, girl. I will call you later, Brandy, to check on you," Katrina told her.

"Okay, Katrina. Thanks, sis, for bringing over the fruit and snacks. I really appreciate it."

"I know," she said.

Katrina left to go straight home to cook dinner for her husband. It was not a special occasion, but Katrina felt good and a little different apparently because she put on some old school jams playing her oldies on her stereo, bought some white wine, and had a candlelight dinner prepared and placed on the table for the two of them. She even had a "Your Special" card she had bought at the store earlier. She added her own words, giving it an extra special touch. She planned a special night for them. She sang and snapped her fingers as she listened to the songs while waiting for her husband to arrive. She was so excited about their first baby.

Gary planned to tell his wife about his affair with her sister. He had been thinking really hard for the past months about how he was going to say it. He had it in his head. He was so nervous, but he knew he had to, at least before she found out by someone else in her family. Gary was on his way home to his wife.

Getting there, he was surprised to see the candles lit, dinner and wine placed on the table, and his wife singing to the oldies but goodies. He couldn't possibly tell her that type of news right then. Walking in looking around and smiling, he grabbed her hand and started singing and dancing around to the music too. Seeing the joy and glow she had and singing like she was the artist herself, he never got around to telling her. He thought, *Forget it. I'm not going to say anything. We have been quiet about it for this long, so why saying something now.*

He twirled her in circles slowly, as her stomach looked like it was about to burst. After dancing, they both sat at the table to eat, having a candlelight dinner, with his wine and her apple cider. Their evening was romantic. After eating their romantic dinner, he took their plates back to the kitchen and came back with two glasses of ice-cold water for them to drink. Afterwards, he took her hand and walked her to the bedroom straight to the bed. They both lay back on the bed cuddling up with each other watching TV. He then slid down to the foot of the bed grabbing her feet to massage them.

One thing led to another, and before long, he was sliding up her leg with his tongue. He spread her legs and went in between. It was during her second month when they last had sex. When she became three months, they just stopped because they wanted to get past her first trimester. Her stomach just seemed like it got bigger. He pleasured her with his tongue. That made her want more than his tongue. Her hormones were kicking in. It had been six weeks, and she wanted to have sex. He wanted to have sex too, but he was afraid of going in too deep with her being as big as she was. He didn't want to hurt his baby.

"Are you even sure this will be okay?" he asked.

"I don't see why we can't. Just don't go in too deep." Gary licking Katrina's pussy left her body tingling; she wanted more.

"Let me get on top first." She didn't care how big her stomach had become; she was about to make it work. She couldn't reach down there of course, so she had him put his penis inside her. As soon as he put it in, she began riding it. It didn't take her long to cum at all. She wanted to be fair, so she lay down on her back, so he could get back inside her.

After the first few moments, it wasn't that she felt any pain, but it was uncomfortable. She thought she would try lying on her side just to see if that was going to make any difference, and it did. It actually felt much better. It was feeling so good that they forgot she was pregnant for a moment. He had to catch himself.

"Babe, I'm sorry," he paused. "Are you all right?" he asked.

"Yeah," she answered back. "Dang, babe. You can't go fast and deep like that. You're going to have to slow it down a bit."

He proceeded to continue to go in, but he went in gently and kept it steady and slow. At that very moment he couldn't control the feelings because he was having an orgasm raging through his body. Gary thought he had more in him, but once it had softened, he eased out of it and lay beside her. Then, they both went to sleep.

The next morning at eight o'clock, Katrina woke up to him in the kitchen cooking breakfast. Katrina really didn't have much planned for the day besides going to the doctor, but that wasn't going to be until three that afternoon. Until then, she was going to relax. At about eleven, Brandy called her and asked if she wanted to go to lunch. Katrina didn't have to think about it; she just told her yes.

"Well, what time did you want to have lunch today?" Brandy asked her.

"Well, you know our doctor's appointments are not until three, well three and four o'clock."

"Ok, how about I come pick you up about one?" Brandy asked. Katrina looked up at the wall clock to see how much time she had to get ready before one. She mumbled to herself, "Okay, I have two hours."

"Yes, that's fine, sis," Katrina told her.

Both sisters going through their pregnancy at the same time was fun for them. It was a way to spend a lot of time together with the different outings they would go on. They shared the same doctor's office and the same doctor's appointments. After they had lunch together, they left the restaurant and went straight to the doctor's office. They also shared swollen ankles, aching backs, and thoughts of different baby names.

Both sisters later on in the pregnancy decided to breastfeed and to use the same type of bottles and same brand name diapers. They were so excited. They couldn't stay out the stores shopping. They had it bad, but it was normal for them to tell their men they would be right back. They left to go to the store, but they ended up at the mall. Every time Katrina saw a baby, she was oohing and aahing. She couldn't wait until her baby came.

They had an appointment every two weeks and instead of going to lunch on one particular day, they had a Lamaze class to go to. After eating the big breakfast their men threw down together in the kitchen that morning, the women knew they were going to be full until dinner. When they were out, they were not paying attention to the time; they were so caught up in what they were doing: "shopping." It wasn't something they had made plans to do that day. It just happened, and they almost forgot about the Lamaze class their doctors wanted them to check out.

Their men, of course, didn't see any use for the class; they were not trying to be dragged along to a class that was going to teach them how to breathe. Being Katrina's and Brandy's first baby, they really wanted to try anything they could. They wanted to make sure the breathing, the positioning and everything was going to be in the best interest of their babies.

Katrina couldn't believe she still had two and a half more months to go. Brandy had just made nine months. Time was ticking, and they were ready. They couldn't wait for their daughters to be born.

Meanwhile, Katrina's and Brandy's pregnancies had them both feeling very uncomfortable when they slept or sat down, but with their Lamaze class, they were able to learn different techniques that could help them to be in a more comfortable state. However, days later after trying out the techniques from the Lamaze class, Brandy was still uncomfortable most of the time because she was due to give birth soon. While Brandy was lying around doing nothing, Chris was handling everything he could since the last visit to the doctor when her doctor placed her on bed rest. On the other hand, the techniques were helpful to Katrina; she enjoyed going to their Lamaze classes.

Gary and Chris had a lot of work to do handling and trying to take care of everything for their pregnant ladies; it was always funny to Katrina and Brandy to see the two of them in action. At any time, Brandy could go into labor. She had reached her due date. One night as she was going to bed, she began having pains in her stomach that made her very uncomfortable.

Five o'clock that next morning, it was about that time. She began to have contractions more frequently; she was feeling the pain hit her too often. Chris started counting the minutes watching his watch every time she made a noise of pain. Once the pain started coming every five minutes, they knew it was about that time to head to the hospital. Brandy called her mom and dad to tell them she was getting ready to go to the hospital because her contractions were coming too often. They told her they would meet her there. On the way to the hospital, her parents called Katrina, letting her know her sister was in labor.

Katrina quickly started preparing to leave to go see her niece born. She tried to take Gary along with her. He showed no interest in wanting to go. He had continued to try to not be in the same area as Katrina and her sister. But, she didn't let him get out of that one. She wanted him to show her baby sister support with her and Chris' new baby. Katrina was so excited and couldn't wait to see her. Brandy was about to give birth in her own private room, where if she wanted to, and she did, she was able to have her whole family inside with her.

Her mom, dad and Chris were already inside the room with her, but the moment she heard her sister's voice before Katrina entered the room, she felt a pain, not a pain from the baby but the secret she held from her for so long. After walking in, Katrina nudged Brandy on her arm.

"Hey, sis. What's up? Ms. Brandy. Ms. Brandy," Katrina said as she leaned down to give her sister a kiss. "How is everything going so far, sis?"

"I'm at eight centimeters right now," Brandy said.

Following the voice of Katrina, Gary spoke to Brandy. "Hey, Brandy."

She hesitated before she spoke. Then, Brandy said, "Hello, Gary." Shortly after, her contractions continued to come; she was screaming, so everyone surrounded her to show support in welcoming her baby girl into the world.

The moment Brandy's baby was born, Chris stood there cutting the umbilical cord after she came out. She had a head full of dark curly hair. She was so light skinned that she almost looked white. Chris was smiling happily, as a proud poppa. He would go crazy to know the baby was not his.

As soon as the baby was born, they all gave her the nickname "Curly Sue," because of all the dark curly hair she had. The baby already had a nickname before an actual birth name. Brandy ended up giving her daughter the name "Paige." Seeing Paige's face for the first time left Chris speechless for a while. He stared without taking the smile off his face. When Chris was able to speak, he told Brandy, "I'm so happy and so very excited, Brandy, to be raising our child together. You both mean the world to me."

Brandy didn't know what last name to give Paige. She didn't know if she should give her Gary's last name. She knew if she did, her sister would kill her. She didn't know if she should give her the last name of the one who thought he was her dad. She couldn't figure it out, so she just lay there as her sister held her baby in her arms while staring into her eyes. As Katrina held her niece Paige, she stood by her mom as they both stared into her eyes.

"Hey, Mom, look at Paige. She looks just like me when I was a baby."

"Baby, we have strong genes," her mom told her.

Katrina walked and held Paige. Katrina and Brandy's parents along with Chris left for the cafeteria to get food for everyone.

Katrina never thought anything of Gary's being over there talking quietly to her sister as she watched from across the room. It had been a while since Gary had spoken to Brandy, so he took that moment to talk to her.

He whispered to Brandy, "Take care of yourself and our baby. If you need anything, I mean anything, just call me. Just please take good care of my princess." Then, he mumbled, "She's so beautiful. She looks just like me."

Reading his lips, Brandy told him thank you. Gary looked down at Brandy making strong eye contact. "Brandy, I'm sorry for everything." Brandy, seeing all the joy her sister was having with her baby, wished she could have told her the truth a long time ago about her husband. She fought with herself about hiding the truth. She was so shameful of what it all had become.

Brandy's daughter looked too much like Gary. The question never was asked, and no one seemed to have wondered. But the two who knew had their conscious eating away at them; they were tripping.

Two days later, Brandy and Paige were both released from the hospital. As they prepared to leave the hospital, Chris parked the car he just bought for them out front, so they wouldn't have too far to walk. He had a big pink ribbon with a bow wrapped around the car. He wanted to surprise Brandy with a cool little car he bought from his boy. Chris only gave him a thousand, but they agreed on him giving his boy monthly payments until he paid if off.

From their first day back at home, Chris made sure when she

woke up the bottles were already made for the day along with Paige's diaper being changed.

"Look at her ear. Watch, my baby is going to get lighter as time goes on," is what Brandy would say to everyone in her family that came to visit her and her baby. At the top of Paige's ear, there was a mocha tone. Brandy always made that statement in front of Chris, so it would seem more believable, so he wouldn't have any doubts. Everyone but Chris *obviously* knew babies don't get lighter; they get darker.

They had a visitor almost every day. Brandy saw Chris as the happiest and proudest father. He was working and able to support his family. Everything he talked about was always for the benefit of their family. Brandy was going crazy in her mind. Having thoughts of when she was having sex with both men. *Hmmm, maybe it could be Chris'*, she thought.

Brandy started going through denial. She wanted a DNA test. She called Gary at a time she knew he would answer her call- during his work hours. Even though she felt in her heart 99.9 % that Paige was his, she just wanted to make sure or at least, she was hoping he wasn't the father.

After speaking with Gary, they were both on the same page about finding out if he was for sure Paige's father. They both agreed to go half on the fee of $500 dollars to get it done. Three weeks later was the soonest they were able to have their appointment. They waited patiently until then. They couldn't wait to see what the result will be.

Just a few days before their appointment, Brandy called Gary as a reminder of their appointment. She didn't want any excuses. When they talked, Gary asked if he could come over to see his princess.

"Sure," Brandy said. Once he got there, he thanked her for letting him come over to see his baby girl on short notice.

"Oh, no problem," she told him. "It was good timing. Chris just left not too long ago." Gary came over and surprised Paige with plenty of gifts from bottles, diapers, clothes and toys. Gary stayed and played with his princess with the new stuff he had bought her. Paige was happy and full of joy playing with her daddy. Brandy didn't expect it because he didn't mention anything over the phone.

Paige was like a wiggle worm when she saw him. He held her and played with her. She couldn't stop cooing and smiling. Brandy stood off and out the way and let them have their time together. She saw the joy and the happiness in both of them. He was so good with her. For the time he could spend with her without any one catching on, he was a real good father to her. He couldn't stay long. After spending time with Paige, he gave her a kiss and a hug and headed out.

When their appointment date came up, they met each other there, taking Paige along with them and paying the fee of $500 dollars. Sitting down, all three of them had their mouths swabbed by the doctor with a cotton ball on a wooden stick. She then placed each stick of cotton in its own individual envelope with their names on them. After that, they left the office. The hardest part was waiting two weeks for the results.

Katrina had been doing everything she could to help Brandy and Chris with her niece, as much as she could with being so close to her own delivery date. She also babysat her niece, so Brandy didn't have to pay a high cost babysitter while she worked. Brandy had just got a position at a health clinic doing front office medical and back office medical assistance. Meanwhile, Chris was trying to finish his schooling.

Katrina was so proud of them both for what they were trying to accomplish. Katrina loved seeing her baby sister happy, and she was happy Brandy had a man in her life who really cared about her, who really wanted to see her succeed in life to become something.

When Brandy got off work, she went to go pick up Paige from Katrina's. After Brandy and Paige left, Katrina went into the kitchen with her hubby. She took some food from the refrigerator she had in there thawing since earlier. She was about to start their dinner.

"Babe, you look exhausted."

"I feel exhausted."

"Why don't you go and lie down. I'll take care of it."

"Babe, are you sure?" she asked.

"Yeah, babe. Don't you worry about it. I'll handle the dinner, and when it's ready, I'll bring your plate to you." She grabbed Gary by the neck, pulling herself closer to his face to give him a kiss as she whispered, "Thank you."

"Oh, no problem. You go lie down." Katrina waddled out the kitchen to go lie down. It was a long day for her, and she knew she had overdone it. Gary stayed in the kitchen preparing a meal for the two of them. When he brought her the food, he had it looking good and smelling good. He brought the food to the bed where they both sat next to each other to watch TV and eat. She leaned over to give him another kiss. He just wanted her to relax more and be comfortable.

Getting closer and closer to the date as days went on, she began to walk more up and down their street in the early mornings. Gary would walk with her to help her start contracting early and to make the delivery go smoothly.

She knew she wasn't really supposed to drink coffee, but one week away from going into labor, Katrina was ready to have her baby. She made some all black coffee, and yes, that made her contractions come more. By that next morning, Katrina began to have pains in her stomach. She waited to see if they were going to stop; she didn't want to have to call Brandy to pick up Paige for a false alarm.

When the contractions were coming every two minutes, she knew it was time. Still not wanting to call her sister to leave early on her second week at her new job, Katrina called their mother Deborah. She immediately came over to get her grandbaby and to help Katrina to the hospital.

Katrina was indeed in labor. Her family and some of Gary's family all met at the hospital. Brandy and Chris showed up when Brandy got off work. She wanted to show Katrina sisterly support. Katrina was only having contractions and was not ready to push yet. She was sitting up while she was talking to everyone, but after sitting for five hours, her pain was getting more intense. Her contractions were hurting her, and her screams and shouts were getting louder. Her pain was getting stronger and stronger. She was finally ready to push.

Everyone was in position. Gary was looking, and he could see the head. He began to panic. He yelled, "It's coming!!" Katrina was doing great; she was screaming in pain but doing great for her first childbirth and with no medication.

Gary and Katrina named their 6 lb. 9 oz. newborn baby girl Simone. Simone looked identical to Paige when she was first born. Everyone, not just Katrina, thought the same. The two seemed to look just like Gary. Their skin color made them look more like him, along with the texture of their hair.

Still no one really said anything. The looks were given, but still no one questioned. "The Johnson family has some strong genes," their mother said. Off to the side of the hospital room as they sat, Chris asked Brandy in a voice only loud enough for her to hear him, "Why doesn't my daughter have my features, my nose, or something?" he whispered.

Chris never mentioned anything of another man. But from time to time, he asked her why their daughter did not look like him. In the beginning, no one paid any attention to how Paige had none of Chris' features until Simone was born and looked identical to her. Paige looked more like Simone than Chris, down to the color of their skin.

Gary and Katrina took their daughter home to her already put together room just two days later. They would wake up at 2am to feed their precious baby girl. For Katrina, getting used to being a new mom was joyous. Gary was a proud father, making bottles for their baby, while Katrina changed the diapers. He would then take his daughter and change her into dry pajamas. He would wrap her in her pink blanket and sit and rock her in the rocking chair. She would coo in his arms. Katrina saw he was great with their baby. For them, figuring out what she wanted through her cries was something to get used to.

Some nights, Katrina couldn't figure out how he was able to figure things out before her about their baby. It was like he had experience or something. Some days when Simone wasn't sleeping so well, Katrina was up at 4am when she had only three hours before she would have to leave for work. Gary would always offer to take over. She observed how good he actually was with her; there were no worries there.

With the help of her husband, Katrina was able to manage the adjustment. When Gary would get off from work, he couldn't wait to steal some kisses from his baby, kissing her head and her cheeks and underneath her neck. Underneath her neck was her ticklish spot. He always loved to see her laugh. When he arrived home, he always took Simone from Katrina for a little while to spend time with his daughter.

Some days later, Brandy had a missed call on her phone. Pushing the button to see who it was, she saw it was the doctor. She dialed the number back, and they told her she could come and pick up the DNA results. On her way driving to the DNA clinic, she called Gary to let him know the results were back, and she was on her way to pick them up.

"Oh, cool," he said. "Call me when you leave there."

Brandy drove the freeway to get there faster to pick up the results. When she retrieved them, she left the envelope closed until she got back into her car. When she got into her car, before she pulled off, she opened the large envelope very slowly and pulled out the papers. She took a deep breath and read the results; it showed Gary was 99.9% the father of Paige. She cried because she already knew he was by how much she looked just like him with the same skin tone, facial features and good hair. Paige didn't have Chris' Indian side at all, but Brandy was hoping the test was going to say something different. Brandy sent Gary a text message telling him she was leaving the clinic and was on her way home. He told her he would stop by the house when he got off work.

Chris wasn't going to be there; he had to work on a few of his friends' motorcycles, and he wouldn't get back until late. So Gary coming over when he got off work was not going to be a problem. Brandy replied right back to his text saying okay.

Brandy didn't want to tell him the results over the phone. She wanted him to see them for himself as she did. Once Gary got off work, he shot straight to Brandy's to see the results. Upon his entry, he gave her a peck on her nose. As the door closed, she passed him the envelope. Gary stood in the living room area looking down at the papers as he read the results. That was something he already knew the answer to, but the confirmation made it that much better. After a while, Paige heard her daddy in the living room; she woke up, and he began tickling her and playing with her while she sat in her bouncing chair. Paige started cooing and smiling at her daddy.

He was excited seeing her right then. Brandy smiled seeing her baby as happy as she was. He picked her up. Whenever she saw her daddy, she always started kicking and smiling. She kept squealing in his arms.

Being the father of Paige and now just having Simone, Gary continued to be the best father for his daughters. Who knew how long the secret would last? Gary was planning to keep it a secret for as long as he could. He figured maybe Katrina would never find out. Always being a man to take care of his responsibilities, he didn't know how he was going to do it, while keeping everything a secret. But a secret like that- he had too.

Chapter 4
Who's the Daddy?

Although Brandy just had a child with her sister's husband six months ago, she knew that was as far as their relationship was going to go: he would only be the father of her child. She knew even if she wanted to, she couldn't have a future with him. That is why she always dreaded the every other week visits going to see him, so their daughter could spend time with him.

Gary made sure every other Saturday, on schedule, he saw his Curly Sue. He was never late. At the same park, sitting at the same bench was where Brandy always found him, right next to a blanket that was already laid out behind him with a picnic basket and a bag of toys and books. Seeing them coming always made him happy. To him, his daughter looked like she was getting bigger every time he saw her. As he looked at her, he told Brandy, "Look how big she has gotten since two weeks ago."

Gary always greeted Brandy with a hug and a kiss when they met up, right before they sat down on the blanket. He always asked her the same question before his full attention was given to Paige.

"You miss me, Brandy?" And just like always, she looked up at him as she rubbed her fingers through her hair. Then, just like always she asked him, "Why do you always ask me that?"

"Because look at us," he would respond to her as he looked directly into her eyes. Brandy always responded by looking down at their daughter and pointing at her saying, "She is why we are here, not because of any feelings I have or do not have for you."

Although Gary had to secretly see his daughter, his only concern right then was seeing her and her smiles, hearing her laughs, playing with her, and even reading baby books to her even though she always looked like he was talking crazy talk. Even though she was only six months old, he knew she was listening, and just seeing her happy made him feel good.

Brandy and Gary's daughter was a very happy baby. Paige didn't cry much, unless she was hungry and had a wet diaper. Other than that she was very good. Gary never liked letting Paige go when the visits came to an end, but when he did, she cried sometimes and that was always the part of the visit he didn't like- the leaving part.

Once a month, as the visit came to an end, Gary would pass Brandy an envelope of money. That was something he did and had been doing since Paige was born because he had to, with no strings attached. When Gary left, he always went home to his wife Katrina being the one she had always known him to be.

When he arrived home, Katrina always had a bottle of ice cold water waiting for him on the kitchen counter. She always knew that's what he needed when he came from jogging in the park. After she had Simone, she and Gary went back to their everyday sex and candlelight dinners. Their marriage was back to normal. Gary had also been showering her with daily gifts for a while. Gary was doing what he was doing out of guilt. Every day, he came home feeling like shit, but he hid it with a smile on his face. His lies were for sure eating him up inside badly.

Gary had been making his sales, so Katrina didn't have to work so many hours as before nor on the weekends. Damn near every night, Katrina felt Gary's penis warm her insides, which always seemed to get started by a simple massage to his neck. A massage she would do with both of their shirts off while rubbing her breasts against his back as she gave him a massage. Katrina had missed the feeling of him warming her up. He had missed the moans and making passionate love to his wife. Lately, she was in the mood almost every night for it, and that made him a happy camper.

On the weekends, they enjoyed their time. Even if they did nothing, it felt good to spend that time together. But, it almost seemed like their weekend went by too quickly. On Monday mornings, they headed out to start their day. Everything was back to normal with them.

Brandy had grown to love Gary, but she was truly in love with Chris. Never once had she ever thought of loving two men at the same time, one whom was already taken by her sister. Chris had been everything she had ever looked for in a man. She couldn't bare the thought of breaking his heart by telling him any differently about the baby. Paige saw him as no stranger. He was just daddy; she always went into his open arms. She loved Chris. Chris loved seeing his little girl get so big in her growing stages, which were coming and going by so fast. He could not express his love enough.

Chris and Brandy had a birthday party to start planning for. They only had two months before their baby girl turned the big "one year old." *The months are coming and going by so fast,* Brandy thought. *Today, Paige turns ten months old.* Brandy had Paige also calling Chris daddy since she was able to talk. The only one who knew the truth about things was Gary. Chris had been so excited ever since Paige's birth. He had told everybody about her. He was such a proud father. Brandy always just stared at him as he told people. She watched or heard and felt bad inside each time because she couldn't tell him the truth from the beginning. She thought a time or two to admit and tell the truth and stop keeping things a secret, but she did not want to steal his joy. And, her truth couldn't come out. She wanted to tell, but she couldn't.

Chris had all the parenting stuff planned out to a "T." He was real good at it, from taking Paige to daycare, playing with her during her play time, cooking for her and just doing any and all a father does. Some days Brandy felt like she wasn't the best woman for him, seeing how great and adorable he was. And as time passed, Chris still had a question he wanted an answer to.

He had taken out an old photo album, to look back at old pictures of his daughter when she was first born and at the rest of Brandy's family photos. After looking through the pictures, he went over to Brandy to show her pictures he had taken out the book to show her his daughter looked more like her niece Simone, like they could be sisters.

Brandy thought fast and said to him, "Chris, as Paige gets older, you will start seeing a resemblance of you." What she feared most was him leaving when he find out the truth. Brandy really wasn't in the mood for the conversation he was trying to have with her. She would rather listen to him talk about sports than that. She felt he was over-exaggerating the situation. So, she sat in the rocking chair and dosed off to sleep. Chris noticed it was becoming a routine of hers when he asked those types of questions. But her falling asleep or beating around the bush with an answer never put him at ease either.

Meanwhile, when Gary was able to have an excuse for his whereabouts, he would take Paige to different places each time, like to the zoo to see the animals and to the museums. He tried switching up because he always took her to the park.

Paige liked the Looney Tunes characters, so Brandy and Chris bought Looney Tunes decorations from Party City: the tablecloths, plates, cake plates, cups, and grab bags. Paige was about to be Looney Tuned out. Preparing everything for the party was a lot of work. Brandy was always lucky to have a big sister like Katrina who was always a big help to her. Her mother came to help out too.

Once they both got there to Brandy's apartment to help her, she was glad she had more help. Brandy thanked them both for coming to help out.

"No problem," they both told her.

"Sis, what do you need me to do?" Katrina asked.

"Katrina, if you could place the tablecloths over all the tables, I would appreciate it," Brandy told her. So, she did. Her mother helped herself with the food. They were expecting a lot of family over for Paige's first birthday.

Once two o'clock came, the party started. Brandy, Chris, Katrina and Deborah were all running around like chickens with their heads cut off, going back and forth from the apartment to the back of the apartment where they were having the party. Katrina didn't tell her sister, her mother nor Chris that she had ordered a character. She ordered Tweety Bird. Everyone was shocked and surprised when a gigantic Tweety Bird joined the party with them.

As she sat watching her daughter, Brandy's butt vibrated. She reached around her back grabbing her cellphone from her back pocket. She looked at it. It was Gary. The message read, "I'm sorry, Brandy. You know I'm not going to be able to make it. Hope you guys have fun. Give my princess a kiss for me. See you both next Saturday."

Everyone was having fun at the party with the face painting, jumping in the jumper, and messing around with Tweety Bird. After the party was over, Katrina and their mom stayed around to help her with all the clean up as well.

"Whew! That was a lot, but Sis, Mom and Chris, we made it through," she said looking at them all.

"Yeah, we sure did," Katrina and Deborah responded.

"Thank you guys so much. I couldn't have done all this by

myself," Brandy told them.

"I guess I see what I have to look forward to in four months," Katrina said.

Katrina figured she had better start planning and buying stuff then towards Simone's party, to get a head start, instead of waiting to the last minute.

Since Gary couldn't make the party, he celebrated Paige's birthday by taking her a small cake to the park the next Saturday. He also brought gifts with him for her as well.

A week later, Gary planned an outing to the zoo with his wife and their daughter Simone. After seeing how much fun his other daughter Paige had when he took her a few weeks ago, he knew he had to take Simone too.

The morning of the day they planned to go to the zoo, the day was perfect. It was hot and beautiful outside that Saturday. Katrina had not been to the zoo since her childhood days, and that was going to be their daughter's first time.

Getting to the zoo that day, they all had a lot of excitement going on. After walking around for an hour, Katrina and Gary were already hot and tired. Katrina insisted they stop for a little snack break. So, they found a cool resting area in the shade that had a table and a bench. They rested there, ate some snacks they had brought with them, and drank a bottle of water. They were having fun so far looking at all the different types of animals. After the zoo, they went home. They were all zooed out, so they all went to bed early.

The next morning, the three of them went to eleven o'clock worship service. The preacher preached a good sermon, and they were glad to see so many people join church that day.

On the way home from church, Gary thought about planning a date night for just the two of them. Later that evening, he set things up for the next Saturday. After making sure Deborah was able to watch Simone for them, he made the reservations for dinner.

Once Gary got off work that Saturday, he went home and shaved and took a shower for the dinner date he had all planned out for them. Katrina had already left even before he got home to drop Simone off at her parents' house. Once Katrina arrived back home from dropping off Simone, he kissed her on her lips and gave her a hug.

"How was your day, babe?" he asked her.

"It was good, but I'm glad it's over. How was yours?"

"It was good, but our night's about to be even better," he smiled.

Katrina had already taken her shower before dropping off their daughter, so all she had to do was get dressed and straighten her hair. After sliding on her dress and her heels, they both were ready to go. They left the house and were on their way to dinner.

When they entered the restaurant, their presence turned everyone's heads. Although Gary had a smile on his face, he knew they were really looking at his wife because she looked beautiful in her elegant dress.

"Good evening. I see the reservation is for two?"

"Yes, it is," Katrina responded back to the host.

The waiter escorted them to their table. As the two were seated, the host handed them both a menu. As they received the menus, the host placed napkins in front of them on the table. In minutes, they were ready to place their order.

While waiting for their food to be brought to them, they took sips from their water glasses and talked. As Gary watched Katrina, he realized what he loved about his wife. It was her laughter and her smile. It just did something to his soul. That is why he enjoyed nights like that, to take her away from work, Simone, and her family, just to have time to do nothing but to enjoy herself for the past few months like they used to do.

During their conversation, the topic of Simone's birthday came up. It was coming soon, in a month, which was actually right around the corner. The food finally came, and the two ate. As they sat and ate, Katrina was eyeing an elderly couple that sat beside them. They still looked happy, and they were on a date night too. They looked so cute. Katrina knew in twenty something years down the line that would be them. She thought that was a beautiful thing to see.

After an hour, the two left. Stepping outside the restaurant, the night was cold, so Gary took off his coat and wrapped it around her, even though she had her own coat on. They stood in front of the restaurant waiting for valet to bring their car.

After returning home from their date night, one thing led to another. Then, his body was all wrapped around her body. The kissing and taking off their clothes came about; then, the two flopped onto their bed as they were still kissing. They began making hot passionate love. Things started off slowly; then, it got a little wild and crazy in the bed. He turned her around, and he went in her from behind, as he began grabbing hold to her long hair until she started feeling cum surging into her body.

After finishing up, they got out the bed and made their way to the shower. Once they were out the shower, they both went to sleep, so they could wake up early for church service in the morning.

That next morning they made it to eleven o'clock service and right after the service, they chatted for a minute with their pastor and with a few members of the church and then they left. Katrina had Gary make a stop by the grocery store on the way home because she needed to pick up a few items to go with her Sunday dinner.

Once they made it home, they changed from their clothes and put on something a bit more comfortable. Katrina then headed straight for the kitchen. She was making a meat loaf, mashed potatoes, collard greens, macaroni and cheese and cornbread.

After their dinner was done, hours later they all ate and chilled around the house. Katrina didn't find herself relaxing too long; she always found something more to do around the house.

She had got Simone a week worth of clothing out for the daycare and began ironing all her clothes for the week. After the ironing, she was beat, so she had taken a shower and laid down beside Gary. Simone joined them in bed and began watching the movie with them until they all fell asleep.

That Monday morning, they dragged out the bed getting ready, but once they all got up, they got ready and were ready to start their day. Every day of that week for them was going to be a busy day, Katrina and Gary had to finish up some shopping, getting the last bit of stuff for the party. They bought Mermaid everything. That was the theme for Simone's first party.

Saturday was coming in just a few more days, and it would be Simone's actual birthday. On that Friday, Katrina had taken cupcakes and ice cream to Simone's daycare. Katrina was happy that her daughter's birthday fell on Saturday, Saturday December 14th was the day of her party.

That morning, Katrina cooked a lot of food for the party. Everyone whom they invited showed, even kids and adults they didn't expect but Katrina had so much food it was still enough for everyone who showed. They had a jumper, a cotton candy machine, a popcorn machine and music. Simone had a blast at her party and everyone else that was there did too.

Now all they needed to do was make it through Christmas, which was in ten days. All they needed to do was get a few more gifts and they would be done.

On Christmas day, everyone met over Deborah and Ricky's house for Christmas dinner. Everyone arrived between the hours of one and two, and all the food was already done. The food was self-serve, so everyone was able to make their own plates as they arrived. All the kids were happy to see each other. They played with their toys, and some rode the new bikes they got for Christmas. All the fellas were inside the family room watching the basketball game, and all the women were full of conversations and laughter in the living room. They all enjoyed themselves like always. Everyone started leaving Deborah and Rickey's house around eight o'clock that night.

The next day, Gary told himself for the next six months he planned to work hard. He needed to sell some houses. Birthday parties and Christmas had "broke the hell out of him."

In six more days, New Year's Day would come, but neither Gary nor Katrina made any plans. They just wanted to stay in that year. When it came, they treated it like any other day. They made no resolutions; they only thanked God for allowing them to see another year.

It was about work, work, work with them and raising their daughter. Katrina stayed busy working. Gary was back to his old routine with the daily calls, checking emails, talking and meeting with clients to view different houses. He hoped to close some deals, along with looking daily for potential clients.

When summer time approached, there was still no slowing down. Gary thought he would be able to until Katrina had an intense conversation with him. During their conversation, she mentioned to him how he needed to keep at what he was doing because the bills were not going to stop or slow down at all. She didn't want to hear any excuses. In between work, they did manage to hit the beach here and there during the week. After the summer, for months it was about improving, getting better and work, work, work.

A year had passed, and Chris and Brandy wondered where the year had gone. It was that time again- Paige's birthday. She would be turning two years old. They thought about doing something different for her, so they just needed to decide what that would be.

Now that Paige was older and about to turn two soon, Paige and Gary's outings were just the two of them. She was talking really well and was able to run around everywhere, so he didn't need to have Brandy along all the time. He really enjoyed his father time with her, which he rarely had. He really loved his baby girl. He often felt very bad about the whole thing because he would never have an answer for his daughter about why she couldn't bring her cousin Simone with them.

He felt bad having to lie all the time to her; he hated his circumstances. He knew one day all this was going to blow up in his face. He just didn't know when, but he always hoped that day wasn't the day. He planned to hide it until he couldn't anymore. He tried acting normal about it around Katrina by acting as though Paige was just his niece too. Unfortunately, that just didn't work out for the brain. The affair, early morning sex with Brandy, Paige, and passionate sex in the car with Brandy kept clouding his brain. The situation was impossible, and something he just had to deal with.

Chris and Brandy decided to have a princess party only inviting nine of her cousins to spend the night for Paige's Princess Slumber Party. That night, all the girls came over with their pajamas on, but once Brandy got everyone settled in, she had all the girls change into the princess gowns she had bought for them. She had also bought ten tiaras and ten pairs of heels pink, blue, and purple heels from the dollar store. The girls looked pretty all dressed up. She polished all their fingernails and toenails. They danced and ate pizza. They ended the night watching *The Princess and The Frog*.

The past couple of months felt like they had gone by too quickly for no reason. Thanksgiving was near; it was in three months, and as always, dinner was going to be at Deborah and Ricky's, the house where mainly all the holiday functions took place. Deborah contacted everyone three weeks before Thanksgiving and told them it was going to start at one o'clock in the afternoon on Thanksgiving Day.

On Thanksgiving Day, Katrina and Gary arrived a half hour early. As soon as they walked into the kitchen, they saw the food they had smelled when they rang the doorbell. They made a tiny plate, just to grab a bite to eat until they ate later once everyone had arrived. Deborah and Rickey cooked all the food and only asked if everyone could bring the deserts. That was simple and easy for them; they all did what was asked of them to do. All the family came, and they enjoyed themselves as always. That's what the Johnson family did all the time.

After a few months of planning, the day was finally there that Gary and Katrina were expecting family over for their daughter's birthday dinner party. She turned two years old that day. They couldn't believe it was her birthday again.

"It's her birthday again. I feel like we just had her party just months ago," he said.

Katrina looked at him. "I know right? Tell me about it," she told him. "Man, this year just came and went."

They both began to make sure the house was clean and a fresh roll of toilet paper was already in the bathroom. Katrina didn't want to hear Gary's mother say, "You guys don't have any tissue."

Then they checked the dinner, to make certain the different dishes tasted how they looked. Normally, he would just help out a little in the kitchen, but that wasn't the case anymore. The guilt he had kept him in the kitchen without even being asked for help. Katrina was shocked, so she disappeared into the living room to make sure everything was looking good.

The dinner party was scheduled to start at three o'clock, but Deborah, Katrina's mom, showed up early. As she walked in, Gary and Katrina both greeted her with a smile. Deborah walked in and gave them a hug and went straight for her granddaughter. Simone was happy to see her grandmother. Deborah looked at Katrina, "Katrina, she is getting so big!!"

"I know right," Katrina smiled. "Look at her, Mom. Miss Two years old today."

Deborah chuckled as she looked at her granddaughter. "Katrina, what are you feeding my grandbaby?"

"Mom, she eats everything. That's her doing."

Deborah looked down at Simone. "Is that true, baby," she asked softly. Simone smiled and nodded her head yes.

It wasn't long before it was three o' clock. Shortly after, a knock sounded at the door. Katrina was headed to the door, but Gary stopped her and told her he would get it. Gary approached the door wondering who was knocking at the door and if it was Brandy. If it was, he wanted to quickly tell her to tell Paige not to call him daddy and that it would be okay to call him by his name. He opened the door, and it was Chris and Paige at the door. Brandy was not there. He seemed a little disappointed.

"What man? You're not happy to see me?" Chris asked him. Gary quickly played it off by laughing. Then, he threw in a joke. Gary greeted Chris with a man's handshake when he entered. Paige was in his arms asleep. Gary was concerned and asked where Brandy was. He wanted to know if she was coming over too. Chris told him that she was going to make it, but she would be coming late because she had to work. Chris asked Gary where he could lay Paige down. Chris began walking her towards the couch.

"Oh, bro, you can lay her in Simone's room upstairs," Gary told him.

"Oh, cool. Thanks." Chris followed him up to Simone's room. After laying her down, they both left the room. Chris showed Gary a baggy of some of that good marijuana. The two went back down the stairs and out to the patio. They took a seat at the patio table and began chit chatting while the ladies were in the house. Chris pulled out his rolling papers from his front pocket and start rolling them a joint. The two continued talking as they were polluting the air with smoke.

After a while, Gary just so happened to look down at his watch and noticed they had been back there almost an hour already. When the guys went back in from smoking, they headed straight to the pots on the stove. They both began sniffing the food that they were ready to eat. Neither of them paid any attention or noticed more guests had arrived. It was Simone's friends and their parents from her daycare. The men were ready to eat.

Katrina called Gary and Chris into the living room to introduce them to the guests that were there. After they were introduced, Gary whispered in Katrina's ear asking her when the food was going to be ready. Katrina told him as soon as her sister got there.

Gary walked back over to Chris and asked, "Chris, have you talked to Brandy yet?"

"Yeah, I did. She said she's on her way, but she's stuck in traffic."

"Well, good as long as she's on her way," Gary was happy to hear that she wasn't still at work. Chris pulled out his phone and called Brandy again to get an update on where she was. After the third ring on her cell, "Hey, babe," she answered.

"How far are you now?" he wondered.

"I believe I'm about twenty-five minutes away."

"Okay, babe. Step on it and hurry up. Katrina's not letting nobody eat until you get here."

Brandy laughed. "Okay, babe. I'm trying to drive as fast as I can," she told him.

Once Brandy showed up, everyone was ready to eat. They set up for everything and the cake design was perfect. Katrina did her thing. She had decorated her butt off. The music was playing, and kids were dancing, while some of their parents were off to the side playing a card game. Everyone was having a great time, especially Simone. With everyone there to celebrate her turning two years old, she was having a blast.

After a while, Brandy started to feel some type of way watching Gary and her sister. As things were looking all good, she knew the real. Brandy felt she knew her sister's husband better than she did. Katrina knew the old Gary. However, Brandy knew the new one.

Later, after everyone sang happy birthday to Simone, Brandy was ready to leave. After singing the birthday song, the guests received their candy bags, and everyone began leaving. After the house cleared out and everyone went home, Katrina started throwing trash inside the trash can to clean up just a little. Soon, she noticed Simone was asleep on the couch. She wasn't surprised to see her fall asleep so fast. Her baby girl was worn out.

Katrina then went into her bedroom. She put on her lingerie and was ready and waiting in bed for her husband. When Gary went into the room, she was looking hot just as he liked her. They both were happy that everything turned out great at the dinner party and that it was over. Lying down beside each other, they began kissing and that soon after turned into love making.

The next morning, she woke up and made breakfast for the three of them. They didn't make any plans for the day, except to relax and get some rest. They planned to enjoy what they had left of the weekend. That weekend, Gary had plans to meet up with Brandy on Sunday, at the same park, at the same spot, at the same time.

As always, she made it there after him. Once he saw his daughter and Brandy, Gary was from ear to ear with smiles. Gary gave his daughter a big hug and kisses to her face. The three went and sat on the blanket that he already had laid out on the grass. As soon as they sat down, Gary went into the basket he prepared for them, and he pulled out a bag of sliced apples and gave them to Paige. She took them and ran off to the slide. It wasn't until Paige ran to the slide that Gary and Brandy had the chance to talk by themselves. This alone time gave them time to talk until she got back.

"So, how have you been, Brandy?" he looked over and asked.

"I've been okay and you?" she asked him.

"I've been good," he said sounding so unsure. "So how have things been with you and Chris? He still not making love to you like I was making love to you," Gary grinned.

She couldn't even say what she was about to say. Her mind began to have memories of their past together. It was so clear in her mind like it was happening again. After he said he had been good, she wanted to know why he sounded like he did as if something was wrong. Brandy wasn't expecting him to ask what he had just asked. It made her instantly forget what she was about to say. She looked at him with a look that said, "Really?" But she was thinking, *Yeah,*

Gary. You were good. As she thought it, she thought, *Yeah, Gary, you were really good, but Chris is good too.* She blurted out, "Yeah, he does."

He looked at her and asked, "How so?"

She was not about to go into details about how good Chris made loves to her. Brandy stared down to the grass, and then she got up and walked off slowly to the restroom. She had begun having thoughts. That was why she excused herself from him to go to the restroom. As she was walking off, Paige ran back over. Brandy asked her if she needed to use the restroom because she was walking over there, but she said no quickly and ran towards her dad.

With the thoughts that were still racing in her head about that unwanted situation he had put her in, she took longer to go back. She had many things she was thinking about. When Brandy did finally go back to where they were sitting, Paige and Gary weren't there. When she turned around to see if she saw them, she spotted them at the pond feeding the ducks. She walked over there and saw how much fun Paige was having feeding the ducks. But, it was definitely time to leave the pond when the ducks began getting out and were trying to following them. They ended up walking back over to the blanket and began talking.

As they were talking, they also began eating the food Gary had bought for them. Brandy and Gary sat next to each other side by side, as Paige sat opposite them facing them. Gary's hands wouldn't obey her when she told him to stop. Brandy wished he would stop, so she could eat her food in peace without him bothering her. She wanted him to stop before something ended up happening. While they were eating, random people and random couples kept walking by speaking, smiling and looking as if they were a couple. Neither of them liked the part where other people thought they were a couple. Although Gary did not like it, that didn't stop him from rubbing on her.

They both realized they both had been stumbling over different things that would normally be a success to them and what they did in the past just may have something to do with it. Brandy came up with the conclusion that trying to live life with the situation hanging over them, nothing good was ever going to come out of any situation.

Gary looked at the time on his cell; then, they began wrapping the visit up. Shortly after, they left the park. Gary went back home and took a shower to act as if he was sweaty from jogging or something. Then, he lay under Katrina. The three of them carried out the rest of their weekend.

Sunday night at about seven o' clock, Gary went to gas up both cars, while Katrina stayed to put away the dishes and to put Simone to sleep. Gary left to go gas up his car first; then, he came back to pick up Katrina's car. Once he was done, he headed back home. It was getting late, and they were looking forward to a busy work week. Actually, the next few months would be busy.

The next day when Gary came home from work, he told Katrina about one of his clients he had earlier. He didn't mean to lead the married couple on when he had showed them a house that they really wanted. He made the mistake of telling them they could get the house. He told them it was going to be guaranteed, but the bank ended up not even qualifying them for it. After telling them the bad news, the wife cried because she really thought she was going to be able to get the house. Gary's client "the husband" saw the pain and madness in his wife's face while looking at her cry.

"So what did you say after that?" Katrina asked him.

"Well, I couldn't say anything. I wasn't expecting her to cry."

"Babe, you can't guarantee your clients something that you really can't get for them."

"I know. So I just told them both I was sorry."

They ended up accepting the apology he gave. He learned from them never to make a promise to any of his clients.

Gary and Katrina were not in a race, but they were running neck and neck on their sales. They continued for months doing really well. They both remained busy, but they were still meeting up for lunch. They still did that daily.

Once things slowed down with work, they both sat down at their house one Saturday morning looking over everything they did over the past six to seven months. A whole year has passed already and Katrina had something to prove to Gary. She proved to him he could make his sales with hard work; he must put in to get the results he wants. Everything was fine for them. Life was good. There were no complaints.

Gary loved his wife, and he loved how she showed him constantly that she cared and didn't mind going as far as she had to, to make things go well for them. He, at times, felt he was ungrateful when he had it all right at home, and instead of being ungrateful, he began to feel that he should have been appreciating her more like she did him.

One day, Gary had taken a day off from work. Katrina had already left to take Simone to daycare. Gary was ready to start his Monday. He turned the computer on. As Gary waited for it to load up, he went to the fridge and grabbed a beer and went back to the computer. Gary began scrolling the internet, looking at different suites to take his lovely wife for the weekend.

After Gary found the perfect place to take her, he called Deborah to see if she could watch Simone that weekend. Deborah didn't have a problem with it at all. After beer number two, Gary called up his boy Mikey to see if he wanted to go to the bar and shoot pool and have drinks. He didn't know Mikey was off that day, but everything worked out perfectly. They both were off, and Mikey wanted to go with Gary to the bar.

As soon as the two made it to the bar, the first thing they did was order shots of Hennessey. After their first three shots, they began shooting pool. Halfway through their pool session, a conversation came up about affairs and women not being satisfied. That little conversation had him thinking. Leaving the bar, on Gary's way back home, he thought he would whip up some dinner and have it all ready before his wife and daughter got home.

When he got home, he looked in the freezer to see what he

wanted to cook. There was a pack of chicken breast, Tilapia fish and a slab of pork spare ribs. *All three sound good,* he thought but he knew he should probably cook the chicken breast. Gary took the chicken breast and thawed it out inside the sink with cold water. As the chicken was thawing out, he started the pasta. He also started boiling a pot with eggs for the salad. Gary called Katrina ten minutes after she was off work.

"Hey, babe!" she answered.

"Hey, what are you doing?" he asked.

"Driving to pick up Simone."

"Okay, cool." Then again he said, "That's cool."

She wondered why he asked when he knew that was her routine after work. "What's up, babe?" she asked.

"Nothing," he said.

"Well, what are you doing?"

"I just got done cooking dinner."

"Oh, how sweet. What are you cooking, babe?"

"I made chicken breast smothered in cream of mushroom, pasta, salad and croissant rolls, but I wasn't going to actually put the rolls in the oven until about ten minutes before we were ready to eat, so they would be fresh out the oven."

When Katrina and Simone walked into the house, Gary already had their plates already on the dining room table. All they had to do was walk in, wash their hands, and have a seat. The three sat down and enjoyed their dinner. During dinner, Gary told Katrina what he had planned for them for the weekend. She was excited to get a break and time to themselves by themselves.

"Oh wait! Saturday is Paige's birthday party," Katrina blurted out loud.

"Babe, you sure? Damn for real?" he asked.

"Calm down," she said as she looked back while walking away from the table. Gary had already paid for the whole weekend for the suite. Katrina looked at the calendar that was hanging up on the wall in their bedroom. Looking at the calendar, she saw that her niece's birthday was the following Saturday, so that meant they would not be missing her birthday after all. For a quick moment, they thought they were going to have to miss it.

Later that night, Gary ran her bath water and volunteered to bathe her. After he bathed her, he grabbed her hand to help her out the bathtub. He then grabbed her body towel and dried her. Next, he walked her over to the bed and told her to lie down. He got a bottle of lotion and gave her a full-body rub down; he wanted to make her feel relaxed.

After taking care of his wife, he then hopped into the shower. After he got out, he put on lotion. Next, he put on his boxers and got into bed. They kissed each other good night. Gary fell asleep before Katrina. She lay right on his side with her eyes closed trying to go to sleep too, but she couldn't sleep. She got up to use the bathroom. When she came out and looked at her husband fast asleep, she was tempted by his body. She went over to the bed and slowly got down on her knees and began kissing his back and giving him light massages to his body. After a while, she rose and whispered into his ear, "Babe, you sleep?"

He began moving; then, he said, "No." He turned his body over, and she crawled slowly over his body naked and began kissing him in his mouth. As she was on top of him kissing him, the both of them knew what was coming. He lifted up and pulled off his boxers. The kissing continued, as their bodies heated each other's, and they began making love.

After they were all sweaty and tired, they just laid there in the same spot. Then in minutes, they fell asleep. The next morning, they both were up early ready to start their day, hoping the week went by fast.

"How did you sleep, babe?"

"I slept good and you?" he asked.

"I slept pretty good."

After getting dressed and getting their things ready, they all left. Just like they wanted, the week went by quickly. There it was Friday morning. Now, if only four o'clock would come quickly.

After work, they met at the house to get the tote bags they had packed the night before. They checked the house one last time, making sure all windows were closed and locked. They turned the alarm on before leaving out. Then, they headed to the suite for the weekend. Once they arrived, the first thing they did was change into their swimming clothes to take a swim. After spending time inside the pool, they got in the Jacuzzi. The Jacuzzi made them both feel more relaxed. Shortly afterward, they went back up to the room. The plan was to enjoy their three-day stay with plenty of relaxing, sitting poolside, enjoying the Jacuzzi, and telling each other why they love each other so much. Gary intended to keep his wife happy; he felt as long as she was happy, he would be too.

The next morning, they woke up to their anniversary day, with the sun shining through the window. They went down to get the complimentary breakfast and then for an early swim. It was just the two of them. Gary had a thought to tell Katrina to take her suit off, but he knew she would have gone off on him, so he figured he would save his thoughts and fantasy for the room.

Getting back to the room, her eyes widened with surprise at the bubbly champagne poured in the two glasses, the dozen rose petals spread all over the bed, and chocolate-covered strawberries sitting in an open box on the dresser. Tears dripped off her chin.

The next morning at eight o'clock, she woke up to him on the phone ordering breakfast for them from room service. After breakfast, they just relaxed for the remainder of their time there.

That night before getting back to the house, they had to pick up Simone and prepare for another work week. On Monday, when Katrina got off work, she picked up Simone, and they went to the mall to go shopping for Paige's birthday. There were so many things to choose from, but they ended up getting her a Leap Frog computer to help stimulate her learning. She also bought her an outfit and shoes.

Chapter 5

The Birthday Party

It was Saturday, August 25, Paige's third birthday, and Brandy planned a nice party for her daughter. She had invited all Paige's friends from the preschool she just started three days ago, along with their family and other friends who lived in the apartments. This birthday was going to be Paige's first birthday party that Gary would attend. On Paige's first and second birthday parties, he gave Brandy reasons why he couldn't make it. He made up for his absence by giving Paige a small birthday celebration with only the three of them at the park during their visit just days before her initial party. For the celebrations, he bought a small cake.

From the R.S.V.P.'s, Brandy knew it was going to be a large group of people coming. She cooked a lot of food, so they wouldn't run out of anything. She wanted to make sure if they wanted seconds or thirds, there would be enough for everyone. Katrina had come early to help Brandy set up everything. Thank God because without Katrina, the party may not have started on time.

All the guests were enjoying themselves by dancing to the music and eating. The kids were jumping in the jumper, and there were latecomers entering with gifts in their hand. Paige was playing with her friends, and then she saw her daddy come into the play area from the side gate with balloons and bags of gifts. She quickly ran to him. He figured he could drop in for a minute to show his face and leave.

"Daddy! Daddy!" she said as she reached up to him for a hug. Picking her up, he gave her a kiss and a hug and showed her bags filled with gifts and then he told her to go play. Katrina turned her head quickly and saw her niece running to go play, but all she saw was her husband with bags of gifts in his hand. She didn't see Chris.

She just knew she heard her niece's voice saying, "Daddy!" Daddy? She could have sworn she just saw Chris inside the house. She wondered when he had time to leave when she had just seen him. He would have had to walk past her to go outside. All she saw was her niece Paige running back with her cousin and her friends away from where her husband was walking. He was just getting there. She was thinking, *I know I didn't hear what I thought I heard.*

"Hey, Brandy. There is Paige's daddy," Jordan said when she saw him from a distance making his arrival.

"Shh!" Brandy raised her finger to her lips to silence her friend from opening up her big mouth. That was supposed to be their secret.

"Oh, yeah. I forgot. I'm sorry," she whispered to Brandy. Brandy knew she shouldn't have told Jordan anything. Katrina wasn't too close to the backyard entrance, but she was close enough to hear her niece Paige call her husband daddy. Gary hadn't even seen Katrina yet. She saw him before he spotted her. She walked around the building, going all the way around to play it off. Katrina was helping her sister put up the games on the walls of the apartment building for the kids.

At first, Katrina thought it was cute for her niece to call her uncle 'daddy.' Then she thought, *Awwww, it's probably nothing. She's only three years old. She doesn't know.* But then, she noticed when her niece saw and spoke to Chris' brothers who came about thirty minutes later, she called them by their names and not by 'uncle' nor 'daddy.' Katrina grew curious then. Her mother saw the hostile look in her eyes. She knew Katrina was about to act a fool.

Katrina was always easier to read by her face than Brandy. When she saw the look of rage on her daughter's face, she quickly checked to see if anything suggested any type of threat from anyone towards Katrina. She didn't see anything out of place, so she didn't see what the problem could be. She didn't want Katrina to do anything to mess up her grandbaby's birthday party. She hurried and got to Katrina quickly.

"Katrina, what's your problem? Are you okay?" her mother asked her.

Katrina looked at her mother telling her, "No, Mom. I'm not okay. There is something I need to ask Brandy about."

"Well, can it wait until after the party?" she asked her.

"No, Mom. This one can't wait. I need to talk to her now."

"Katrina, what is it about?" A serious look settled on Katrina's face. She didn't say a word; she just walked away. Her mother pulled her back. So, Katrina told her mother what she just heard her niece say.

Deborah let her go and told her, "Oh, no baby. It must be some type of misunderstanding."

Katrina wanted to at least make sure it was just a misunderstanding. Walking past her mother, she walked straight to Brandy. She asked Brandy what was up with her niece calling Gary 'daddy.' Brandy just looked at her silently.

Without any hesitation, she had to tell her. It was now already out; no more keeping it a secret.

"Katrina, me and Gary had been having sex, and I ended up pregnant with Paige." Katrina didn't believe Brandy was as serious as she was. "But, it's not happening any more, of course. It happened when I was staying at your house," Brandy told her.

Gary walked up and stood by them. Brandy and Gary were both standing there looking stupid. Katrina glanced at her mother who stood right in the middle. She looked shocked by what she was hearing. She saw the hurt in her daughter's eyes. She realized that wasn't one of Katrina's spontaneous acts. She wasn't trying to mess up her sister's day.

Katrina said, "I beg your pardon." Gary stood there and watched the tears fill up in Katrina's eyes. Gary knew there wasn't an explanation he could tell his wife for what he had done. He knew at that very moment his marriage was in jeopardy. Katrina got so close to Brandy's face, spit was accidently spraying on Brandy's face.

Katrina looked at both of them, "How could you both do this to me?" She asked them right in front of everybody. They both stood silently.

"Let's get this shit straight!" Katrina shouted with anger.

"You mean to tell me you've been having an affair with my sister?" she asked Gary. He couldn't form his mouth to answer. She stared into his eyes pointing her finger towards his face. "I knew it, and when I asked that question to the both of you at different times, you both denied it and had me thinking I was the one tripping."

Brandy told her, "K, you need to step back some. You are way to close up in my face. You're spitting and shit."

At that very moment, Brandy and Gary had no choice but to confront the situation. Brandy just didn't want to do it in front of the family, their friends and the kids who were all looking, trying to see what was going on. No one had caught on to Paige calling Gary 'daddy,' except Katrina. Brandy wanted to go inside and talk. But, all hell broke loose when Katrina saw her attempt to walk away.

Before she could have fixed her lips to say, "K, let's take this inside and have a talk." Katrina wasn't trying to hear anymore.

"Where the hell do you think you're going?" Katrina shouted.

"Let's go inside," Brandy told her.

"Fuck no! We are not going anywhere." Katrina didn't care one bit who was around. She didn't mean for the kids to have to hear what they were talking about, but she was too pissed off and hurt to even care. Katrina was mad as shit. Even knowing how Brandy was before, Katrina gave her the benefit of the doubt, thinking she changed. *Damn, look what happened,* she was thinking to herself. She should have known Brandy was trouble. Katrina was embarrassed.

Before anything could be settled, Katrina quickly started socking her sister in the face, with both her hands- nonstop. Gary pulled her off Brandy, but when he let her go, Katrina started kicking his ass too. She started socking him in his face as hard as she could; she had no plans of stopping, at least until she was tired of swinging her arms. Katrina was socking them and slapping them both very hard- smackkkk, smackkkkk. The sound of it was so loud. Gary knew everyone heard it. Once she struck, she couldn't stop.

"Katrina! That's enough," her mother said.

Finally, she stopped. Katrina had to calm herself down from the rage that had come over her. Because Katrina hit her so hard, Brandy tumbled slightly backwards. She did not fall, but if she had been hit a little harder, she would have. Gary stood there looking crazy, holding his face. Katrina didn't feel bad at all for socking and slapping the hell out of both of them. After all, they both deserved it. Really, their asses deserved more than that, but being at her niece's birthday party, she was trying her best to keep it PG.

"Simone, come on!!" Katrina said while crying.

Her mother said, "Katrina, I'll bring her home later."

"Okay," Katrina told her mom, as she walked over to her give her a hug and telling her goodbye. She then walked over to Simone. She kneeled down to give her daughter a kiss and a hug. Then, she left the party. Katrina was so devastated that she left out crying. She sat in her car and cried. She never imagined she would be in a situation like that one.

Some of their family members who heard it all were looking at Brandy differently. She only stayed outside in the back because it was her daughter's party. Her mother stood there ashamed of her daughter's actions. Gary wanted to chase after Katrina and beg for her to come back or at least to stop and talk to him, but he felt it would be best that she cooled down first. Sitting in her car feeling lost, Katrina was confused, hurt and surprised at them. Chris was shocked. He looked so confused and was speechless; he went into the house away from everyone. Katrina went and parked her car down the street, so they would think she left. Not too much longer after she left, Gary did too. Because everyone heard what happened, he was feeling uncomfortable.

She sat from afar and just watched. She saw her sister walk Gary out to his car. She couldn't believe they were talking like they were the married couple. Katrina had the thought of starting up her car and running them over without stopping. She thought hard about it. She didn't because she knew someone might see her and call the police. As Gary got inside his car to take off, after talking to Brandy, Katrina decided to follow him. She felt like she was going crazy out of her mind. At that moment, she had thoughts of killing him.

She stayed two cars behind him, so he couldn't see her. Wherever he turned left, she turned left. Wherever he turned right, she turned right. But once his ass got onto the freeway, she didn't want to lose him, so she ended up getting right behind him with her high beams on. When Gary exited the freeway, so did she. She guessed by that time he realized he was being followed because he started driving faster down narrow streets and cutting quick corners. She was right on his bumper. She was ready to hurt him. She stopped caring if he found out it was her right behind him. She stayed on his ass.

Not driving the speed limit, she kept looking back in her rear view mirror making sure she did not see the police. Posted speed signs read 55. She glanced down at her odometer, but kept her focus on his car. She noticed she was going 80 miles per hour; she wasn't trying to lose his car. As they approached a yellow light, he made a quick U-turn. Quickly, before the other cars coming in the opposite direction of traffic got near, on the red light, she bust a U-turn too.

When everyone finally left the party, Chris came out the room still hurt. He was sick to his stomach from crying so much. After fighting his pain, until he couldn't fight anymore, he went and talked to Brandy. Before he could say anything, she began apologizing. He told her, "I know she's not my daughter by what I just heard today, but I am her father, and I'm not going anywhere."

He didn't want to pretend, but he didn't and couldn't leave her. He was already attached. Brandy was, of course, shocked to hear him say that, being as hurt as he was. The only thing he couldn't do was stay engaged to her. He asked for the ring back. She gave it back, but she gave it back with an attitude. She was the one he had wanted to marry, but not anymore after what he learned. He called off the marriage. Chris was tripping out about how close he came to marrying her, without knowing she had been having sex with someone else: her sister's husband. And, the baby was not his. Everything was crazy as hell. Brandy felt really badly for lying to him and depriving him of something he wanted badly, and even doing what she did with Gary.

Gary made that last sudden turn, and she lost him. After Katrina lost him, she made a stop by the store to pick up some new locks and keys to change all the locks once she got home. After she changed the locks, her phone rang, and she saw it was her mother.

"Yes, Mom? Are you outside?"

"No, I was calling to tell you I'm bringing her home in the morning. Are you going to church in the morning?"

"Yes, we are. Why?"

"Are you going to the eleven o'clock service?" her mother asked her.

"Yeah," Katrina said.

"Okay, then I'll bring Simone about seven."

"Okay, Mom."

"Love you, baby. Sorry about what happened."

"Mom, stop it. I don't want to talk about it right now."

"Sorry, baby."

"No, it's okay, Mom. Love you and see you in the morning." They hung up. After what happened at Paige's party, she decided it would be best to take off her wedding ring and put it up high in her closet in a box, so that is just what she did. She knew she was not going to need it any time soon. She started packing all his things into his luggage and sat the suitcases by the front door, so he wouldn't have too far to walk once he got there.

She was never used to living alone with their daughter without him. But it was something she was going to have to get used to. Katrina had the pleasure of canceling the MasterCard and the Visa credit cards they had together. Katrina waited up for him, thinking he was coming to the house. Seeing how pissed off she was, she figured he thought it would be a bad idea. So, she lay down for bed but couldn't sleep from imagining Gary and Brandy sexing together. The visions that kept popping up in her head felt too real to her. She didn't start falling asleep until 2am the next morning.

That morning, Katrina was barely able to get out of bed from crying all night. But, her door bell was constantly being rung at seven o'clock. Her mother was dropping Simone off. After making Simone go back to sleep in her room, Katrina did too. She went back to sleep quickly; she was tired. Again at about 8:45 am, Katrina was awakened. Gary was trying to get inside the house; she heard his keys rambling at the door. He didn't know she had already changed all the locks on the doors. He needed to get in; he almost reacted by doing something stupid from a thought of busting out the windows.

From Gary's loudness, she knew he wanted to come inside their house despite what just happened a day ago. As Katrina watched him, he stood and thought about it for a brief minute. He stood there standing in one place looking down like he was thinking about something; he had his right arm on his hip and his left hand on his chin. She looked down at him from the upstairs window. She peeked from behind the curtains and saw him walk back to his car to sit, but he did not drive off. She guessed he just decided to wait until she opened the door. But, she lay back down; she wasn't worried about him.

At 10:10 am, he knew she would be up in the next twenty minutes getting ready for church. He figured he would sit to wait in the car until she woke up. Looking up at the house, he saw the lights were still off. At 10:30 am, he rang the doorbell; she answered without letting her daughter hear who was at the door, just in case she tried to run to him. Katrina answered as Gary was asking her to come in. She quietly handed him all his things without saying a word to him. He tried to take a step forward to hug her, but she pushed him back onto the porch. Stumbling back, he quickly squatted down getting on both his knees asking for her forgiveness. Looking at his black eye and busted mouth, she didn't know she had done all that.

Gary wasn't sure about what to say to her at that moment besides, "I'm sorry." He wasn't trying to make her any madder. She shut the door and locked it. Leaving there, he, who had never had to stay in a hotel, checked into the hotel up the street. Katrina left right afterwards, heading to the bank on the way to church. She had plans to clean out their joint banking account but the ATM only allowed her to only take out two hundred dollars, but she wanted all of it.

Katrina went back to the car, and on her phone she transferred the funds from their joint account to her personal account. She left him with shit with his old cheating ass. Fuck him.

At the hotel, Gary didn't feel like going anywhere; he just wanted to stay in and lay around all Sunday. He decided to place his clothes inside the drawers and settle in. After placing his empty suitcases in the closet, he flopped down on the bed and closed his eyes to get some sleep. But, he couldn't fall asleep, lying down on the queen-sized bed lonely with a million thoughts going through his head. But, he had some time to think about his bad choices and the mistakes he had made.

After lying down not able to sleep, he tried to find something to watch. He continued flipping through the local channels and the cable channels feeling exhausted. Flicking through the channels, he didn't find any good movies on, just old ass movies. There wasn't anything too interesting, just news and pornos. Not wanting to watch either, Gary just turned off the T.V. and forced himself to take a nap. That evening, he tried to call Katrina, after he got two Coronas in his system.

"Hey, you reached Katrina. Sorry, I'm unavailable to accept your call right now, but if you leave me your name and contact number along with a detailed message, I will be sure to return your call at my earliest convenience." Beep. She sent him straight to voicemail. He didn't bother leaving her a message.

The next day, Gary had a few appointments with some clients to show them some houses he was trying to sell. Before going to meet with his first appointment, he stopped by the house to see if Katrina was going to talk to him. Through her curtains, she saw his car pull up. She grabbed her phone and sent him a text. The text message said, "Leave! I don't want to talk."

Katrina's mind was already made up to not deal with either Gary or Brandy. She hoped he quickly saw her text and left, so she could leave. She was already running late for work and to take their daughter to preschool, but she wasn't leaving until he left. As he walked up to the front door, the text on his phone came through. Without having a chance to ring the doorbell, he left.

Gary called her every day and night from his cell phone or the hotel room phone, but she still wasn't answering. She kept sending him straight to her voicemail every time, and the day he showed up again at the house, she didn't want to see him. For days, she wondered how could *he*, and for days, she wondered how could *she*.

Still going to bed crying and waking up with her puffy hurting eyes, she wondered why he would do that to her. Gary was calling Katrina's cell phone every day begging for her back. She gave him not one response by never answering when he called. He knew with her he needed time to really think about how he was going to get her back.

After a few weeks of calling her and not getting an answer, he decided she might answer if she were to see another number show up on the caller ID. He used a random person's cell phone to call her. She did just what he wanted her to do, which was answer her cell phone. But once she answered and heard his voice on the other end, she became upset.

She shouted, "Gary, why are you calling me?"

"I need to talk to you," he told her.

"It would be best Gary that I don't talk to you or see you at all."

"Wait! Wait! Baby, I have to say something important to you."

Katrina wasn't trying to hear it. She bluntly told him, "You can call all you want, but I'm not accepting any phone calls from you at all." She hung up the phone. But, he was still left with her voice in his head of her calling him to come upstairs just for a kiss or rushing him out the house to get their daughter to school on time and the smell of whatever dinner she was cooking or whatever cake or pies she was baking. The pain he felt from not having all of that was hell. Being brokenhearted, he couldn't sleep; he only drank more.

Some nights, Katrina and Simone would have late dinners. Most of the time, they would be in bed by eight to be up by five or five thirty. Some mornings, Katrina would be up early at two or three in the morning. drinking wine, often worrying about what went wrong. She sat questioning herself; she didn't know if it was her, or if she did something wrong in the relationship. She had tried to be the perfect wife by cooking, cleaning, being a successful business woman, loving and being loyal to her husband, helping produce within their home by working together as a team, and picking up the pieces when he dropped the ball, not meaning for any of it to have affected the intimacy in their sex life.

As she sat and thought about it, she knew it wasn't her. It was just him thinking about himself and thinking with his head, not the head on top of his shoulders, but the other head down there. She didn't see how her heart was ever going to be the same, and for the first time, she actually knew how a broken heart felt.

Spending the past month crying alone every night made her body weak with headaches. Katrina called up her girl Shante, and her girl Shante called their other girl Sharee. The three were on three-way. The three had been friends since high school, but when Katrina got married that kept all their hanging out and partying to a very tight limit through the first years of her marriage. That left Katrina and her girls Shante and Sharee to stay in contact with each other through phone or email.

Now, Katrina wanted to spend some real time with her girls Shante and Sharee. She wanted them to hang out with her at the house. She didn't go to work. She had taken the day off, but she did manage to still get up and drop Simone off that morning at preschool. There were no better people to hang with than with those who knew her best. Hearing in her voice that Katrina was hurting, they were concerned.

Hours later, Sharee called off from work, saying she was sick. Sharee and Shante both paid her a visit. Even at a distance through the years, there still wasn't too much that could be hidden from each other. Between the three of them, they all knew each other too well.

They acted as if they were blood sisters, so it was never a need to ever hide anything. Both girls arrived to her home at the same time and rang her doorbell. Katrina was happy to see them. Once she opened the door and her girls entered, they air kissed each other on the cheeks, and that was when the smile and tears came on her face. They both said, "Awwww," at the same time and gave her a hug, telling her, "It's going to be okay." Just the laughter they began to share was what her heart needed.

Shante and Sharee were truly her loyal friends who knew each other well enough to know when there was a problem with each other, without having to say there was a problem. Having girl time for them always included laughter, drinks and food. After four years, that still had not changed.

Katrina went into her kitchen and poured herself and her girls a drink mix with Vodka and pineapple juice. While she was making drinks, Sharee and Shante began pulling out tomatoes, cilantro, onions, and the last lime they saw in the door of the refrigerator, after seeing Katrina already had some ripe avocados sitting on the counter. They whipped up some guacamole and opened the bag of tortilla chips.

Like always when they got the chance to talk, they began reminiscing about the good old times and what they all were currently doing and whatever plans they had for any new adventures they might have for the future. Just her girls being there made everything start to feel a little better. The girls talked about going out that night.

So later that night while getting dressed, she promised herself when she got to the club she was going to make sure she had a good time. The thought and memory of what he had done to her was painful. Katrina hoped going out with her girls on that Friday night would ease her pain with a little two-step at the club.

She was not trying to bring herself down by thinking about her pain and hurt behind what had happened, but for her to completely get over him was a little impossible unless she met someone. She did not know how easily it would take her mind off Gary or for how long for that matter. For what she was going through, she knew she was going to find it difficult opening up to men. She didn't know how she was going to know if she could trust the person when she talked to him.

After getting to the club, she and her girls went straight for the bar and ordered drinks. Right then, she just wanted to have fun and not think about it. They found a table for three close to the stage. It just so happened, the table was closer to the loud DJ speaker. They weren't too happy about it, but all the tables were already filled up, and it was too packed to pull the table back a little.

Sitting inside a crowded loud nightclub having a good time with her girls, drinking having fun, the thoughts still ran past her mind. Katrina just couldn't believe after nine years, he would have done that to her. They had been married since she was eighteen; she had sacrificed her whole youth. She was feeling stupid and looking dumb when she needed to be out there on that dance floor in the arms of another man.

After the girls' first drinks, they were feeling just how they wanted to feel. The girls were ready to dance. They went out on the dance floor showing out. Her phone kept vibrating; no matter where she seemed to be, it never failed. He was always calling her phone. She looked at her phone and put it back into her purse. She continued having fun. Leaving the club and checking her voicemail, she hoped he had not left another freaking stupid message.

As Katrina listened, she learned yes, it was him again saying, "Baby, please answer your phone. Baby, please call me back. Baby, I'm sorry. Baby, call me. Are you still alive? Pick up!"

She had heard it all, and once again, just like the other night, Delete, Delete, Delete and Delete. She didn't have the time for his games. Her never answering and always pressing the decline button on him never made him give up. He still kept at it every single day. He knew he deserved the treatment she was dishing out to him, if not more.

Katrina still woke up early that Saturday morning for work. Simone was already at her mother's, so she went on with her day after having the best time out with her girls. She knew calling them would be the best thing because they would know how to deal with her pain. When her girls had come over yesterday, they helped put life back into her.

After that weekend, Katrina no longer had a silent house. She would cut the radio on when she came home from work and sang loudly to almost every song, whether she knew all the words or not.

After helping her daughter with her homework, they always had mother and daughter night, painting their fingernails and toenails and watching movies. After Simone went out for the count, Katrina would always lay by the fireplace with a glass of Moscato, while reading a good book. She saved one day a week to go out and have fun with her girls.

A month of her not answering Gary's calls caused him to not see or hear from his daughter and his wife. Gary woke up every morning and left the hotel to drive back to the house. Katrina would be gone already. He noticed she would leave earlier and earlier each day and always at different times trying to throw him off her schedule. Gary was so hurt by how badly he fucked up from doing what he did to the real woman he truly loved. Gary regretted what he had done big time. He continued to call Katrina. She finally answered after a month, but when she answered, he only heard the voice of Simone. He paused in silence and cried. Then, he happily talked to his daughter.

"Hi, Daddy," Simone was happy to finally talk to him. "Daddy, I miss you. Where have you been? Mommy said you're out of town working."

Although he was in town just up the street at the hotel, he just went with the flow of the conversation and told his baby girl, "Yeah, baby girl. Daddy is out of town working. I've been here for a month now. I really don't know how much longer I will be down here, but I'll make sure I keep calling you."

As he got off the phone with his daughter, all he could do was stare at the walls of the hotel room being mad at himself. Gary couldn't take it any more living in a damn hotel when he had a nice big house just up the street.

The next day, after a long day of work showing a couple of houses, he returned to the hotel. He began packing all his things, putting everything into his car. After getting all his belongings in the car and double-checking his room to make sure he left nothing behind, he checked out at the front desk.

Never once did he have any trouble or problems while he was there. All the other guests who were living there too were friendly and very nice. He was just tired of being there and wanted to be back home with his family. Leaving the hotel, he made a stop by the house hoping Katrina would talk to him, but when he got there she wasn't there. After waiting in front of the house for forty-five minutes, he called up his boy Mikey who didn't stay too far. Gary asked if he could stay the night there. He told his boy Mikey what happened for the most part. He hated to talk about it. Mikey told him to come on.

After a long day of work, and it being the start of the weekend, Katrina wanted to go out with her girls to enjoy herself. So, she called her babysitter to watch her daughter. She then hooked up with her girls. Shante and Sharee were the party girls. They went out nearly every weekend, either on a Friday or Saturday night to different clubs.

It was nothing new to them, but Katrina just wanted to have some fun. Katrina wasn't trying to become a party girl. She just needed to get out and not be stuck in the house. She wanted to hit the spot they went to last weekend. There wasn't anything wrong with getting a little loose from time to time. Between her mother and the babysitter, one of them would watch her daughter.

Lately, Katrina had been seeing her sister in the neighborhood because Brandy lived close to their mother's house. When Katrina saw Brandy, she had to fight her and sock her up a few times.

Getting mad all over again every time was beginning to mess up her evening before going out to have a good time with her girls. Every time Katrina saw her sister Brandy, she was fired up with so much anger and pain. She would hop out her car leaving her purse on her front seat and the door wide open. She slapped Brandy very hard on her face and punched her with her fist with her same right hand each and every time. Katrina always dared her sister to hit her back, but she never did. That seemed to relieve a little of the pain each time.

LaShane Moore

Chapter 6
Heartless

Katrina had her mind made up; she was going to enjoy her life with or without her husband's CHEATING ASS. Two months later, Katrina wanted to see Brandy, not to fight with her, just to talk. She wanted to look at her sister while she talked to her face to face for the first time, without actually trying to hit her. Since her niece Paige's party, every time Katrina had seen her sister, she punched and slapped her. Katrina wanted Brandy to see the emotion on her face when she spoke.

All Katrina could think about was how Brandy could do what she did knowing Gary was her life. Katrina wanted to hear from Brandy in person and not over the phone about how she destroyed her marriage, when Katrina was only trying to help her out by allowing her to move in. Katrina wanted to nip it all in the bud and just to get to the bottom of why Brandy had slept with her husband. *No thought. No consideration*, Katrina thought as she also wondered why she found out the way she did.

Once Katrina and Brandy were together, Katrina sent her

daughter in the room to play with her sister Paige. Katrina stood there and asked her, "So, when did all this start?" Brandy took a deep breath.

"Katrina, I don't even know how to start this." Katrina stared at Brandy deep in her eyes. She remained silent and did not blink. Katrina sat down on the couch as they both just stared back at each other. Shortly after just staring at each other, Brandy took a seat on the couch shortly after Katrina did.

"Well, about two weeks after I moved in, I was asleep on the couch bed, and he just got in bed with me and stuck his dick in me while I was asleep," Brandy began.

As Katrina sat there on Brandy's couch listening to her sister talk, she wanted to jump up and sock the shit out of her.

"Damn!" Katrina told her. "That was a bit graphic."

Hearing that from her sister's lips, she didn't have any love anymore for her or Gary's ass. Brandy was shaking. She was so nervous telling her sister what she was telling her. It was hard admitting everything to her. She wished she had followed her first mind years ago and told Katrina when it first happened.

"Brandy, you should have told me that same day. Why did I have to find out like this?" Katrina asked her angrily.

"Katrina, I knew you would have been hurt to find out what Gary had done to me. I'd honestly thought after that first time he was going to stop. I had no idea he was going to do that a yearlong."

"So what, Brandy? Out of respect for me as your sister, you couldn't have stopped him? I mean come on now. That's my husband," Katrina told her. "The first time he did that while you were asleep it wouldn't have been so hard for you to push him off you and immediately tell me."

"Katrina..........Katrina," Brandy stuttered.

"Since it was already in me and after thinking it was Chris doing that, I ended up letting him continue since it was already too late."

"You let him continue!!" she said sarcastically. "Because it was inside of you? Are you fucking kidding me? Brandy girl, I just don't know you anymore," Katrina looked at her and said. "You're saying the most stupid shit out your mouth! That's your best answer?" Katrina asked as she shook her head. "But, Brandy, you have your own man. Why did you have to have sex with mine?"

"I'm sorry," she said. Sorry was not a good enough answer. Katrina slapped Brandy's face, and Brandy hopped up holding her face. Her face went from round to oval shaped real fast. She was mad as she rubbed the side of her face. Brandy regretted telling her about Gary's penis being inside of her.

As Katrina listened to her talk, the thought going through her mind was of them having sex in her house. That made her wonder if they were having sex before that or just after Brandy had moved in. She really couldn't trust shit Brandy said. Brandy had made a bad name for herself within their family.

Even as Brandy's sister, Katrina had no respect for her after what she had allowed to happen. And Gary, her husband, had no respect, no loyalty, and no love for her.

Katrina knew the reputation her sister used to have back in the day when they were younger, but she also knew Brandy had stopped her activity of sexing different men for money or attention. When their dad found out, he ended that quickly. Katrina never once thought Brandy would fuck her husband; otherwise, she would have never let her come to stay.

Katrina told herself from there on out, nothing mattered anymore but her daughter and her work. Katrina wasn't so surprised about Brandy, but she was surprised Brandy had chosen her husband out of all the men to choose from. Her husband? Yeah, she was shocked.

Brandy kept trying to ask for her sister's forgiveness that night, but Katrina had become mad all over again and couldn't come to accept it still. Days later, Brandy was still trying to ask for her forgiveness again by calling her and trying to talk or by leaving messages on her voicemail. Eventually, Brandy went to Katrina's house to talk to her, but she wasn't there. Brandy was hoping she would get lucky and hear her sister forgive her.

She kept calling her. "Katrina, I'm so sorry!!!" Brandy had started to sound like a broken record.

"Katrina, I'm so sorry!!" "Katrina, I'm so sorry!!" is what she was leaving on her voicemail. So for the second time, Brandy went over there again, Katrina finally answered her door after seeing Brandy with her niece Paige through the peephole. It was a shock that Katrina even answered the door for Brandy. Brandy and Paige walked in, and Paige gave her aunt a hug and ran to Simone's room. Brandy quickly thought to say something to give Katrina hope about her husband.

"*He* really really does love you," Brandy told her. "I know it may take time, but you two can work it out."

Katrina couldn't believe Brandy had the audacity to say that stupid shit out her mouth, when her ass was the reason for that shit in the first place. Katrina had too. She slapped the shit out of her ass, and she pushed her down to the floor in the doorway of her living room. She shouted, "It's because of your ass that my marriage is FUCKED UP!!!"

"I told you I was sorry, and it was your husband who did what the fuck he did while I was asleep. I told you!!"

"But you didn't say shit, and you kept at it," she yelled.

"Once again I told you sorry, Katrina!!"

Katrina went charging at her. Brandy quickly got off the floor and ran towards her and pushed her. Katrina fell down a few feet away from the glass coffee table. She got up fast and swung her fist towards her. Brandy, with her quick reflexes, moved Katrina's fist out the way with her left hand and then socked her with her right fist. Brandy didn't want to fight her sister, but she was sick and tired of being hit and not defending herself. Enough was enough. Katrina came back quick and socked her back as she stared her sister in her eyes. The two were fighting like trained boxers. That lasted for a few minutes. Afterwards, they didn't exchange any more words. They were out of breath, so they just stared at each other.

Katrina then told Brandy to leave her home. Brandy called Paige, so they could leave. When she walked out, Katrina slammed the door. Katrina didn't mean for Paige and Simone to hear their crap, but Brandy had pissed her off all over again. Katrina just could not believe her. She just couldn't deal with her anymore. Not many family members were dealing with her either. No one could trust her. The ladies in the family, from the cousins and the aunts, all watched her at any family function they had since Paige's party. No one could trust her around their man.

Meanwhile, Gary was still going over trying to talk to Katrina and work things out. To him, she wasn't trying to do the same thing. Instead, she played it off and hid her emotions. Katrina couldn't and wouldn't talk to him after what he did because she had loved her husband as his wife she by doing everything he wanted. She could not understand how everything she did for him was not good enough.

She felt he was out of his mind to hurt and disrespect her, and then try to beg for her back right afterwards, as if she was about to lower her standards and her self-esteem by accepting him back. He was losing it. She was tired of being the one getting the short end of the stick. In the short time since the day she put him out the house, he had hoped that would have given her time to forgive him and accept him back. But, it didn't. She wasn't worried about him, nor did she care about him anymore.

Months into their separation, she could still hear the desperation in his voice in each conversation they had, but that still didn't stop her from being mad at him nor was she giving into his words. She still told him, "Gary, you are wasting your time." She told him that every time he would come over or call her cell. Still, she never answered the phone, but she would respond to him through text messages. Even though she told him that, he had a comeback.

"Babe, I'm just trying to make things better between us," he says. "Baby, Katrina, let me come back home," he said.

"Well, it's a little too late to worry about us now," she told him. He knew he had hell to pay. She couldn't understand how he thought he could ease his way back home; it wasn't going to be that easy.

But for whatever the reason, getting over him completely and out of her mind took forever to do. She was hurting over something that happened three years ago, but she was glad to have found out sooner than later. Before Gary, Katrina rarely dated anyone. She had been with him since high school. She only had an interest in him at that time and had been with him ever since. She'd knew after their first date, after the tri-school dance at the Hilton Hotel, one day she would be willing to marry him, and they would become old enough to make that decision when they were ready.

Katrina and Gary married each other just a year after high school. They were only eighteen years old. He was her high school sweetheart, and he was the only man she had ever been with to love and honor. Not once before had she ever tried to talk to anyone, not even any of her clients, and they were all wealthy and handsome too. She was always surrounded by rich clients, and most of them were men, but not once had she ever made herself approachable.

Now trying to meet new people on a different level than business felt weird. She couldn't believe she would ever have been without Gary. Questioning men and asking private and personal questions to get to know them was a little different from what she was used too. Being still mad at her husband, it was a little hard for her to connect with other men on that level as she tried not to compare them to him, while not knowing anything about them yet. She had to get over the fact she was only used to him, loving him, or trusting him, especially after what he had done. It was going to be just a little hard to look at anyone else differently.

Chapter 7

Not Wanting Your Love

(Three Years Later)

After not talking to her sister but only a few times in the past three years, Katrina almost didn't care if she ever talked to her again. But Katrina never once took out her frustration or her anger on Paige. She loved her niece so much. To be able to spend time with her, she would have Brandy drop Paige off at their parents' house. When Katrina got off work, she would pick Paige up. Katrina mostly had Paige on the weekends, and she always had something fun planned for the girls.

Simone and Paige were very close; they were the same age and liked all the same things. Being so young, Simone and Paige didn't think to ask any questions about why their family had suddenly told them they are sisters when at first they were told they were cousins. They were confused about that, so they still called themselves cousins. Katrina hadn't broken everything down or told them anything yet. She was waiting for the perfect time and the age when she thought they should know, or when they actually asked for themselves, whichever came first.

When the girls were close to turning seven years old, they became really curious. Their curiosity grew from many people saying they were sisters or they look like twins and others saying they look too much alike. The questions came when Katrina least expected them.

One day while at the grocery store, they were shopping for food for the house and cookies, ice cream and popcorn for the girls. Then all of sudden, the girls began asking questions. It was odd. It must have been on their minds because it came out the blue. Katrina then broke it down and told them what they wanted to know. They guessed that was why they were so close. It always seemed they were more than cousins when they were together. Being the only child of their parents and being together when they were younger felt more like being with a sister, without even knowing they really were sisters. The girls weren't mad at all or shocked; they were actually happy just knowing they were sisters.

While standing in line, Katrina noticed a gentleman that kept looking back at her. She looked behind her thinking maybe he was trying to get someone's attention who was behind her. Looking back, she didn't see anyone interacting with him, so she turned back around. He was still looking at her, and he was trying to get her attention.

"Momma, who is that man that keeps looking at you?" Simone asked.

"Sweetie, I have no idea." But she noticed that he was looking good from afar.

After it was time to place her items onto the check stand, she looked towards the door to see if she saw the guy who was staring at her. Katrina didn't see him anymore from inside the store, but when she left the store, he was waiting for her outside. Once she got outside, he walked up to her sparking up a conversation.

"Hello, beautiful," he said as he grabbed her hand and kissed the back of it. It had been a long time since a man had kissed her hand.

"Hello, how are you?"

"Better now that I've met you," he said. She blushed. He made her one dimple pop out on her cheek. "What's your name?"

"My name is Katrina. And yours?"

"My name is Dameon."

Even up close, he was looking like all that and a bag of chips. He was tall and skinny with a light complexion. He was well groomed with neat corn rolls and a beard. He was dressed in his work clothes. He asked if it was okay if he called her sometimes. She said sure and gave him her number. She didn't bother getting his; she just gave him hers. He was good looking, so when he asked for the number, she gave it. Not knowing what he was really about, she figured what the hell. It had already been over three years, and she hadn't tried to talk to anyone. That was the only way she was going to find out what anyone was about and that was if she met people and talked to them.

Besides her husband and her family, she didn't deal with many people. Katrina had two really close friends who were so awesome to have as friends. So, meeting Dameon was nice; he did not call the same night. She liked that. He waited to call her a couple of days later. When he called, they had an interesting conversation that had her laughing here and there. After talking with him, he seemed intelligent, nice, and funny, with a great personality over all.

As time went on, they began wanting to hear from each other daily. So, they kept calling each other every day in the evening when he got off work. Talking to him a few times a day at first was fine, but then it seemed like he was running out of things to discuss, because at times she caught him talking about nonsense. He always talked about the big name company he worked for. She was impressed by what he was telling her. Only seeing him once so far in a month's time, they wanted to hang out, so they made arrangements for their first date.

After looking through her closet, she ended up pulling out jeans and a blouse to wear. She was actually dreading the first date because that was going to be her first time being with another man since her husband. She put on a pair of fitted blue jeans. They were the kind that looked like jeans, but they were the spandex material. They are called jeggings. She wore them with a white button-down blouse with her white pumps, the ones with gold spikes on the heel area of the shoe. After looking in the mirror, Katrina unbuttoned only the top two buttons of her blouse. She wasn't trying to reveal any part of her breasts.

Dameon sent her the address to his grandmother's house that night because that is where he was and she had offered to pick him up. After picking him up, they headed to a restaurant. He looked nice; he had on blue jeans with a large white design stitched on the back pockets, a black button down shirt and black dress shoes.

The food at the restaurant was great. When the tab was brought to their table, he didn't bother opening it up. She supposed he figured since she was making really good money she would just pay for their tab, or he thought she was footing the bill since she had picked him up. She sat there thinking. She looked at him mumbling to herself, "This man is something else."

She told him, "You have us on our next date."

"Yeah, yeah for sure," he said. Trying to get used to the dating scene, she already had the feeling it was going to be hard for her. Later in the week, they planned a movie date. The night they planned for their date, he called her to say he would pick her up in his blue Tahoe truck between 7 and 8 pm because the movie started at 8:30.

She said, "Okay, see you soon, Dameon." They hung up. For their movie date, she didn't know if she wanted to wear something casual like jeans or a dress. After looking through her closet five times, she ended up wearing a dress and heels. Her curves were filling out perfectly in her dress. She knew she was looking good. She even felt good too.

When Dameon arrived to Katrina's house to pick her up, she let him in, and he wrapped his arms around her trying to give her an affectionate hug. She almost passed out from the overspray of his cologne that overpowered her nose. It had her nose hairs sticking straight up. It almost smelled as if he got off work, changed clothes and just sprayed cologne on.

She couldn't really smell funk, but he did have a stench to him. He was dressed in dark blue jeans. She believed they were the same blue jeans he wore on their first date because she saw the same white design stitched on his back pockets. But that time, he had on a brown sweater and his brown work boots. He looked okay, but she didn't know why he smelled that way. She had on a fitted burgundy dress with the back out. After she grabbed her purse, they left.

As soon as she stepped outside, she felt every bit of the 80 degrees. She didn't realize it was so hot outside because she had been sitting under her air conditioning all day. Looking around, she didn't see a truck like he said he was coming in. He showed up in a white minivan. She didn't like the fact he had lied. Katrina didn't know if he was trying to make himself out to be something he wasn't. But she couldn't focus on that; it was just too hot. It was seven thirty at night, but it was still 80 degrees outside. His air conditioner was not working, and there was not much wind blowing either.

She was glad the theatre was not that far away. Driving to the movies was interesting with the type of conversation they were having. But getting there and getting out the car in the parking lot at the theatre was even more interesting when she saw him reach into his ice chest in the back of the van to get two cans of dripping wet iced teas. She couldn't believe that fool would actually do shit like that on a second date. Katrina chuckled to herself. That shit right there showed her once again how cheap he was. *Oh my gosh! What a turn off*, she thought.

After seeing that, she didn't even want to see the movie. She wanted to turn right around and go home, but because she didn't drive, she thought she would stay without making a scene.

He then put the cold dripping cans into his pockets trying to hide them. Katrina shook her head. She couldn't believe it. Walking towards the theatre, he placed his arm around her waist. Then, she felt him slowly move his hand down to touch her ass.

"Oh, no. Don't do that. It's too soon for that."

"Sorry about that," he apologized to her.

After he paid for their tickets, they went inside and found seats at the top in the middle section. Sitting there, the movie had barely come on, but she was uninterested and still ready to go home. Then, he had the nerve to step out the theatre. Katrina quickly called her girl Shante. After the second ring, Shante answered. "Girl, I thought you were on your date," she asked her.

"I am," she whispered.

"Why are you whispering?"

"We're inside the movies," she continued whispering. "Girl, this mutha fucka is crazy." Shante began laughing.

"Girl, what did he do?" she asked while still laughing.

"Wait, wait let me call you back. I see him coming back now."

"Okay. Bye."

"Bye." Katrina hurried and put her phone back into her purse.

Dameon came back with two clear empty water cups with ice in them. She thought, *I don't know why he brought me a cup.* He started pouring her a drink of tea, but she tried to stop him by telling him, "No thank you. I don't want any tea." But Dameon still poured it anyway. She was pissed that he didn't listen. She sat there not enjoying the movie; she just stared at the screen not even following what was going on. She was pretty much in a daze. When the movie was over, they left walking out towards the car.

He looked over at her. "This turned out fun."

She was in her own thoughts, but she snapped out of them when he said that. "What turned out fun?"

"Our date," he smiled.

"Oh, yeah," she said, but she was thinking, *Yeah right.* As they approached the car, he told her he didn't want the night to end; he wanted to keep her longer. She quickly told him to take her home, telling him she had to be at work early. Of course, it was a lie; she was just trying to end the date early.

She was ready to see her street right then. Once they pulled up in front of her house, she couldn't wait to get out the car. He quickly got out the driver's side to try and run to her side to open up the door for her to be a gentleman, but she was already halfway out the car with one of her feet touching the ground. After walking her to the front door, he tried to follow her in. She stopped him right at the door. She was not having that. He stopped and gave her a hug.

"So, Katrina, when can I take you out again?" he asked her. *Never* is what she wanted to say. But no, she decided to be nice and polite. She took a deep breath; then, she said, "Umm, you can't. I'm fine."

"What did you say?"

"Umm, I don't think I'm ready or cut out for this dating thing yet. You know this separation from my husband is still fairly new."

He probably wasn't used to women turning him down or at least not right to his face, because as he was leaving, he still told her he was going to call her the next day. Katrina was Dameon's challenge. He knew it was probably him sneaking those drinks in the theatre that caused her to not want to talk to him anymore. He knew he sensed a little attitude when he took them out his pocket. He didn't mean to show a bad impression already. He was determined to get her out again. He really was digging her.

With no husband to come home to for the past three years, Katrina spent another lonely night in bed by herself. Dameon sure wasn't about to be her first choice. Going out with her girls every week to the same club and meeting different men had been cool, but she still hadn't found the man to replace Gary yet. She felt it was about that time to try and see what else was out there. Dameon sure as hell wasn't the one. He was cool for conversation, but she wasn't really feeling him.

The next day, Katrina couldn't wait to tell her girls about her horrible date with Dameon. Katrina called Shante to chat with her for a bit to finish telling her what the hell happened.

"Hey, Ms. Lady. How are you?"

"Katrina girl, I'm fine. What about you?"

"I'm good now."

"What do you mean *now*? What happened last night?" Shante laughed.

"Girl, let me finish telling you. For starters, the dude I told you and Sharee I met at the grocery store a few weeks ago, girl, we had our second date last night. That was our last date too." Shante burst out laughing. She knew whatever Katrina was about to say was going to be funny.

"Girl, we were getting out the car and his ass had much nerve to get some drinks out his ice chest. He didn't see me looking at him, and he straight put that shit in his pants' pockets."

"Girl, no he didn't! Not inside his pants' pockets!" Shante laughed.

"His pants were getting all wet. It was so embarrassing, and then when we got inside the theatre, his ass left and came back with two clear water cups filled with ice. He poured me some tea. I told him I didn't want any iced tea, but he poured it anyway. Then, he asked me if I wanted something from the concession stand. I said, 'Sure, some nachos.' He came back in with the nachos, but then he started eating my food with me. I was pissed because I didn't offer him any." Again Shante burst out laughing; she couldn't stop laughing.

"Looks like we need to find you someone else, Katrina," Shante told her. Katrina and Shante began laughing loudly while holding their phones. Once the laughs calmed down, they ended their call.

Days after their date, Dameon kept calling and calling. She

desperately wished he would stop. She couldn't take it anymore, so yes she ended up giving him another chance, but only to talk over the phone, not for any more dates.

Later in that week, Katrina went out shopping for new curtains for her daughter's room and a nice-looking guy stopped her. He asked if she had a boyfriend.

She replied, "No, I don't." He then asked for her name.

"Katrina," she said, "and yours?"

"Greg," he replied.

The two exchanged numbers and talked later that night. And just days later, she invited him over to pay her a visit. When he arrived, she opened the front door for him.

"Good morning, beautiful."

"Good morning," Katrina responded, as Greg walked in carrying a box of donuts and a tray holding two coffees.

"Aww, how sweet of you. Thank you," she told him.

Katrina and her new friend Greg were talking and getting to know each other a little bit more by asking each other questions. They were comfortable, so they opened up to each other. Between each sip of their coffee, they gave each other interested looks. It was obvious they had an attraction to each other. He didn't stay long; he just wanted to hang out with her before he ran his errands.

The next morning, he called her to see what she was doing. After speaking to him for a few minutes, she said she wanted to see him, and he wanted to see her too. So, he went to pay her a visit. The two seemed to be enjoying their time together, and they both wanted to keep seeing each other. When he got there, he walked in with a box of donuts again and a tray with two coffees. Something in the box smelled good, but it didn't smell like donuts. It was a bacon and egg sandwich.

She found it nice of him to bring her breakfast without having to ask him to do so. He left at noon because she had plans to hook up with the ladies for their spa and brunch date.

When Katrina hooked up with her girls, they sat and talked and meeting a nice gentleman came up in the conversation. Uncrossing and crossing her legs, she couldn't keep still nor could she hide anything from her girls.

"I've met someone special," she said smiling. Katrina was looking surprised at how both of her girls were looking at her. "And yes, he's a nice gentleman so far," she said looking directly into their eyes. They were surprised to hear about her new friend, but the conversations continued.

After brunch, she departed from her girls. They all had things to take care of and errands to run. So, they decided to catch up later. By the late afternoon, she was beat, but she still had to go home and prepare dinner for two.

The next morning, Greg came back with breakfast in hand. He was so sweet. After eating their breakfast, he saw her reach to rub her shoulder.

"Babe, you okay?" he asked her.

"I hurt my shoulder last night putting boxes in the pantry. I can hardly move it." He placed his hands on her shoulder where the pain was and began massaging it.

"Damn, babe. I can feel the tension in your shoulder," he said.

Her head fell back showing her smooth neck. Greg thought maybe that was an invitation to lean down to kiss her neck. He began kissing all over her neck. Kissing her tasted sweet. But then, he stopped. It was too early in their friendship to try and go any further. Her eyes made him want her more. He couldn't help himself. Fuck it. He went for it. He began tonguing her down. She tasted so damn sweet.

He raised her shirt, and she didn't have a bra on. He went straight for her nipples. While he was sucking her nipples, she rubbed his baldhead then moved down to his ears. He lifted back up slowly giving her more kisses on the lips. Things were getting too heated. She knew having sex with him right then would be too soon. But she wanted it just as much as he did, and she would rather suffer the consequences later on.

Oops!! Saved by the alarm ringing on his cellphone! It was 1pm, and he had to pick his son up in fifteen minutes. Greg took a deep breath, and they blossomed a bright smile at each other. Katrina's heart was pounding like she had just run around the block twice. It was definitely a sign that she was ready and that they both were ready for whatever almost was about to take place. When he left to pick up his son, he called her back to see if he was able to come back over later.

"Sure," she said.

Greg came back over around 7:30 that night. Her daughter was already asleep by then. Katrina had a movie already set up in the living room for them to watch. He came back with a bottle of Pink Moscato. She was prepared for a great night with him. Katrina went and got two champagne glasses from the kitchen cabinet. As soon as she sat down, he popped the bottle open and start pouring their drinks.

They sat close together on the couch to watch the movie she had found for them. The light was dim, as the two sipped champagne. They made small talk as they watched the movie. She noticed he kept topping off her glass with more Moscato. In no time, she was so tipsy she was slurring her words and was a little loose. He saw her getting loose, so he began rubbing her breasts and kissing her neck. She felt a hot steam on her body.

"Show me where your room is," he told her. He stood her up and asked the question again. Then, she led him to her room. As soon as they got to her room, he lay her down on the bed, ripped her clothes off and began eating her out until she couldn't moan anymore. Then, he went straight to her mouth, giving her a kiss. At the same time, he slid his penis inside of her.

"Wait! Hold up!" she said. He paused. "Wait! You need to put on a condom before you try and put it in," she told him.

"Do you have one?" he asked her.

"No," was her response.

He got out the bed, put his clothes back on, and drove around the corner to the gas station to buy a box of condoms. She was disturbed that he tried to put it in without a condom. He made her uninterested in him after what he tried to do. She felt he just might do what he did to her to other women. She was trying to figure out what made him that comfortable to want to have sex with her without a condom knowing nothing about her. When he came back from the store, she let him in. He quickly took off his clothes and quickly put on his condom when they walked into her room.

She lay there without putting forth any effort, letting him do what he had to do; after he came, she wanted him gone. She couldn't be straightforward with him, so she made up a lie about having to pick up one of her family members from the airport. After he left, she was still disturbed about what had he tried to do.

Later that evening, he called her and apologized for not putting on a condom first. She appreciated his apology. That night, she lay underneath her warm covers thinking thoughts of him while wondering if he was also thinking of her.

Days later, she felt emptiness inside her. She hadn't seen him since the last time he came over, and the last time she heard from him was that night when he called her apologizing. She kept trying to reach him, but she continued to get his voicemail. She decided to just give up and stop trying. Katrina saw that was probably all he wanted anyway. Just when she thought he was different.

Katrina and her girls talked, and they talked about going out. Every day, she talked to Sharee and Shante, and everyday, they mentioned going out.

"Yeah, you just might meet someone better," they told her.

"No, girl. I just want to go out to have a good time." Katrina didn't really like not having a man. Although they would come easy, she just wanted to take her time to get to know them. She was, of course, looking for something real and long lasting.

It was the weekend, so the ladies went to have fun. Stepping into the club, the music was thumping very loudly, so no conversations were being heard by any of them. Getting inside, Katrina didn't feel inappropriate any more seeing that the other women were also dressed to tease, leaving nothing to the imagination having their come-fuck-me dresses on. The ladies headed for the bar, before deciding what they wanted.

A man squeezed in between the ladies asking to buy them a drink. After the nice gentleman ordered and paid for their drinks, he then left the bar. They began looking around seeing the nice crowd of people there, a lot of handsome fellas, and a lot of cleavage showing looking for any man to please. Once they got the alcohol floating through their bodies, they were ready to dance. Katrina, Shante and Sharee went out on the dance floor feeling loose and dropping those hips like they were young out there.

They were looking fly, and they had a lot of the men there mesmerized by their beauty. Dancing by themselves didn't last long before three hot ones walked up from behind them. The three quickly assessed the good-looking guys with their eyes before they began dancing with them. Katrina had the tall one; she thought he was nicely groomed and nicely dressed. Sharee had the short one, but he was taller than she was and had muscles bulging through his sleeves. He too was nicely dressed. She liked him. Shante had the one with all the gold chains hanging from his neck. There were at least three or four chains, a blinged-out watch, and a diamond stud in his ear.

Katrina then tilted her head back on his chest and started dancing. After dancing to three songs, they took a break at the bar. The guys bought the ladies a drink. They sat and talked through two songs; then, they danced their way back through the crowd. Later as Katrina left the club, she thanked her girls for a good time.

Katrina was thinking maybe she should just go out and focus on having a good time instead of thinking she was going to leave the club with another man to replace her husband. Hanging out with her girls every week more frequently in the past three years really showed her the good, bad and different in women and men. They were having way too much fun though, just like the old days before any of them took off in their own direction for college. Katrina had been the first to part the clique way back then, by getting married right when they all graduated high school.

Before leaving the club parking lot, they vowed to each other to never let a man get in between them like she allowed Gary to do before. Katrina had driven to the club that night, but before taking Shante and Sharee home, she had to stop at her mother's to pick up Simone.

The next morning, Simone and Katrina made it to eleven o'clock worship service, and after service, Katrina prepared Sunday dinner for the two of them. They had no plans for the evening besides staying in and watching movies. By seven, Katrina began ironing her and her daughter's clothes for the entire week. Katrina put Simone in the bathtub by seven thirty, and they were in bed by eight. The next morning, she thanked God for waking her and her daughter up. She was ready for another long workweek.

Days later, the girls decided to go out on Thursday night. Shante and Sharee met at Katrina's to get dressed. Katrina, Shante, and Sharee were getting ready for the club, trying out a different night there; Thursday night was Reggae night. Katrina was holding in her hand her little black booty shorts, looking for her royal blue blouse with the back out to match her pumps. She was looking for it like crazy when her cell rang. She quickly grabbed it and answered.

"Hello, Katrina. How are you?"

"I'm okay," she murmured.

She was mad at herself for answering the phone so fast. She didn't even get a glimpse of who was calling. She hadn't heard from him in two weeks.

"I was wondering if I could still see you."

"I don't think so," she replied. He seemed a little startled by her answer.

"Well, why not, Katrina. I've done nothing but show you a good time. I made you laugh and showed you respect. Did I do something wrong?"

Her eyes looked at the phone as she thought to herself- *What good time did you show me?* Not wanting to hurt his feelings anymore, she just told him she had been busy lately and right then it was just bad timing.

"If I did anything to make you feel uninterested, I'm sorry, and if you give our friendship a chance, I can show you I'm not bad at all."

Katrina sat on the phone getting annoyed with him begging.

"How does that sound, sweetheart?" he asked.

"Well, Dameon, that sounds good, but I'm fine. I'll hold on to your number. But I do have to go. You have a good one."

"You too. Bye."

"Finally!! Ughhh!" She couldn't wait to hang up from him.

Shante and Sharee said at the same time, "OMG!!" They chuckled. "Damn, Katrina. You got his ass hooked already. You must have given him some."

"FUCK YOU, GIRL…. I have not given his ass anything. Shoot, imagine if I did. Hell naw! His ass was on some crazy shit. He can go somewhere now." They laughed.

As Katrina was about to give up on her royal blue blouse and find a different shirt and pumps, she found it on top of her laundry basket inside her closet. It must have slipped off the hanger. After the three had finished getting dressed, they looked like models. They were ready for the club.

To their surprise, it was packed on a Thursday night. All the Rastas were out that night. Two hours and three drinks later, they were really buzzed. They were drunk but still able to know what was going on. Katrina, Shante, and Sharee were having fun, still dancing on the dance floor after the last song played ending the night. When the lights came on, they were still dancing. Once people began leaving out, they headed towards the car.

Sharee said, "I actually had fun."

Katrina and Shante said, "Me too, even though I never heard of any of those songs before."

"Yeah, Thursday is going to be our new night," they said.

They all laughed but were all in agreement that Thursday night was going to be their new night at the club. Friday nights and Saturday nights were cool, but Thursday nights were better. Everyone danced the whole night long, and even though it was overly packed for a Thursday, nobody tripped over each other.

After that night, they cleared any schedule they might have had as Thursdays were dedicated to "Reggae Thursdays." After going a few times to "Reggae Thursday," they noticed men were always grabbing them up wanting to dance with them. They did it all in fun, to have a good time.

The last time, after dancing and having a few drinks with her girls, Katrina met someone. The guy, with his bold approach, approached Katrina with a smile. Her girls watched him walk over to her while she was dancing with someone else, place his hands on her waist, and ask her to dance. She couldn't believe his nerve, but his boldness made her go along with it. She could have said no, but he was hot. She liked what she saw. Katrina looked over to her girls.

They were already nodding their heads up and down. She read their lips, which were saying, "Yes, girl. He is fine." They gave her 'thumbs up.' Through the loud club music, he had to whisper into her ear to ask her name.

"Katrina," she replied.

"I'm Mike, good looking," he said.

The Reggae Club and the sound of the music had everyone moving, and everyone's bodies pressed so hard up against each other. They were moving their bodies like they had no bones.

Katrina was out there moving her hips from side to side, and her butt moved up and down with the help of Mike. Dancing with him was making her feel like they were out there making out, and it made her forget she even came there with a problem at all. She twirled her body, moving it like she was a Jamaican herself. She felt a warm feeling go through her body the closer he got to her. The only thing that mattered was she was having fun.

The next week, Katrina went back to the club for "Reggae Thursday." Seeing him back there, showing his interest in her, made her feel more comfortable with him. He bought her and her girls drinks before they went and put a hole in the dance floor. Katrina and Mike were talking loudly to each other, screaming through the music, but they still could barely hear each other even with them being so close together. They stopped trying and continued with their drinks, bobbing their heads to the song that was playing that Mike knew the words to.

She didn't know the words, but it seemed that it was a likeable song because it had the whole club turnt up. The people were dancing out their chairs and jumping up and down. Everyone seemed like they knew the words. When it came down to it, Katrina was completely in control of her own situation. She knew just what she didn't want. Meeting him the first night, sharing a conversation, and dancing the whole night, they, of course, exchanged numbers and started calling each other that same night.

In person, he seemed cool, but over the phone with the questions he asked her, she didn't know if he was a little intimidated by the type of work she did selling houses or what. She didn't want to jump the gun and off the top assume that, so she figured she would give him some time.

A month later the two got together and went out on a date by themselves and had a good time. Never once did he ever try to take advantage of her. Respecting her, showing interest in her, and always showing her a good time was all he did.

He was good looking in the jeans and blazer jacket he wore out to dinner. She was still mad at Gary for sexing Brandy, and she felt like sleeping with Mike that same night.

On their first date, it was just the two of them without her girls. That gave her the chance to see if or what she had been missing was much. During their date, they were enjoying their time. She told him without being too aggressive and forward, "Kiss me." He kissed her for the first time. His lips touched hers, and one thing was leading to another. As she slipped her tongue into his mouth, a warm feeling ran through her body as they were kissing. It made her feel like she was out of space. It was the same exact feeling she felt when they met for the first time when they danced. He slowed her down. He didn't want anyone walking past their booth at the restaurant and see them making out. He said, "We can go on as far as you want later once we leave here."

After the date, they headed to his house. She had total control of what she clearly wanted, and oh yeah, she wanted it. He took her back to his place without first making sure she was even okay with it. She thought he had probably done that before- have a one-night stand. But, she was all over him on their date, so he knew that's what she wanted. She had never had a one-night stand. Because she liked him, she didn't want to consider it a one-night stand. If he was good in bed and if he continued being the type of man she needed, she planned to keep seeing him.

Sleeping alone at night was getting the best of her. She wanted to be loose just for a night. In that heated moment, she wasn't even trying to ask him about any one-night stands or about any other women.

Getting to his home, he invited her inside and offered her a drink, not that she needed more, but it was a polite thing to do. Having a few sips wasn't going to hurt. They began kissing. His tongue entered her mouth as they stood in the living room but everything quickly led straight to his bedroom. Into his room they went. He grabbed her, pulling her closer to him. She lowered her head onto his chest as he began caressing her back as he hugged her. At that very moment, she no longer felt empty inside. It wasn't until that past year that she started regularly wishing for a man to be with on a daily basis, to share special moments with and to have sex with.

To somewhat have that now was cool, different but cool. Katrina slightly lifted her head up to his and started making eye contact as they began kissing. As they kissed, he began rubbing his hands all over her body. Rubbing his hands across her breasts, he could feel through the fabric of her blouse she had no bra on. Her nipples were nice and perky as he touched them. Feeling her nipples as he rubbed them gently, he lifted her blouse up, so he could suck them. Holding her breasts in his hands, he began to suck them one at a time.

She wanted to make wild passionate love since it had been three long months since she had sex but decided she wasn't trying to ruin the moment. So, she went nice and slow letting him lead the pace. It probably was a bad decision to do that so soon, but she had too. She wanted it, and she just couldn't resist. It was definitely satisfying as they made love all night long until the early morning.

The last time Katrina had found herself in someone else's bed, she was barely fifteen years old. It was at her best friend at the time Hollis Cooper's slumber party. She had sleepwalked into her friend's brother's room. She tripped and fell onto the mattress he had on his floor where a male friend of his was lying down snoring. The friend hopped off the bed after she fell beside him. Back then as teens, they both had freaked out.

Waking up the next morning with Katrina still in his bed, Mike slipped out to go make breakfast. He hoped she liked omelets because that was what he had in mind to make. Waking her up when he was done to breakfast in bed, she enjoyed it, and it was so delicious she asked for more when she was done. After eating her second omelet, he drove her home. She had some errands to run for a party she was having later that night. When she got home, she took a shower and got dressed. She was trying to get dressed before her girls got there. They were planning to spend a day of shopping for jewelry.

Katrina and her girls spent all day shopping and eating at their favorite restaurant enjoying themselves like always. Katrina was planning to cap off the evening by hosting a jewelry party at her house. She invited her family and her girls' families and other people she knew, along with friends of friends. It was going to be her second time hosting a jewelry party. The first one she gave last month turned out really well. She believed that one would too.

Katrina planned to host one once a month, as long as they kept doing great. Before the party, she cleaned up, trying to get the house together. There wasn't that much to do, but the front yard was going to be a challenge. The sun had gone down a little, but there were still blue skies out. She wanted to work on her landscaped yard. It had been a while since she had been out there to work on it. Doing it by herself, she could only get out there as her time and as the weather allowed her to. The yard only took an hour to do. Afterward, she took another shower before the party started.

Throughout the day, she thought about Mr. Mike a few times, but she never called him. With him, she knew it was not meant to be. After the night they had last night, she couldn't think of being in a relationship with him, because with him all she could think about was sex. It wasn't about love for real. It was about him meeting her needs. She just tried something different all out of hurt, and she liked it. She thought he was fun to have around, held interesting conversations, was great in bed, was a great kisser, and was very respectful to her. But enough of that, she had to get her mind focused on the party.

Katrina had both silver and gold earrings, necklaces, and bracelets set up on different tables. Everything was setup nicely. In the living room, the jewelry stands held the gold items and the family room had all the silver. The party was very successful. Many of her family members and friends came over to support her. They were very interested in the pieces she had, and they were buying it all up.

She waited days later to call him. She felt it was more lust than like that she felt for him. Nights alone or even nights taking a bath, she thought of calling him, but she didn't. She needed something that felt real. She couldn't believe she was starting to miss him when she didn't see him for a few days. For the past three days, they had been missing each other's calls. After that fifth day, she was sitting in the bathtub of hot water when she thought to try and call him. Katrina called him with the sounds of her bath water in the background. He asked why she didn't let him know she was getting in the bath.

She asked, "Are you saying you want to join me?"

"Either that, or I could just wash your back for you. Whatever you want, I'll do."

Katrina liked the sound of that for sure. "So, did I hear you say you want to join me?" she asked him again.

"I did," he said laughing. "Just joking," he said.

She laughed it off; then, she asked him, "Well, would you like to come over and oil my body down?"

He said, "Yes." She then told him her daughter was already asleep and he could come over, so he came. She lay back soaking in the bath before washing up. When he got there, she got out the bath. She let him inside. They missed each other, so they embraced each other while giving each other a slow kiss as their tongues touched inside each other's mouth. They both went into her room. Feeling his hands sliding over her body with the oil felt so damn good as she lay there. He didn't miss an inch of her body; he made sure he rubbed it all from head to toe. He turned her over onto her stomach to oil her backside. Once he finished, he turned her back over. Then, he raised one of her legs and took a seat on the edge of the bed and then he rested her leg on his knee and began massaging her feet. After he was done with that foot, he repeated it again with her other foot. Mike got up off the bed, leaned down to her and began kissing her, while she grabbed his head bringing him closer down to her face. As she moved his dreds out her face, she felt him slide in.

She heard her phone vibrate on the dresser. After reaching for the phone, after they were done, she saw it was Dameon. Still Dameon was calling her every day. She didn't brush him off all the way, just enough for him to eventually figure she didn't want to be bothered. She had Mike in the picture now keeping her well occupied.

Chapter 8

I'm Not Going Anywhere

Gary was staying just a few blocks from Katrina, at his boy's house. After work, he would make it a point to stop by to see her. He would be there at their house, sitting out front asking to fix things between them, expressing how he was so sorry and how he could never forgive himself for what he had done. And, he said he missed and needed his wife back. When she saw him, she knew changing all the locks to the house when she did that night years ago was best. Otherwise, his ass would have come inside. She still wasn't trying to hear him at all.

Still, the daily calls had never stopped. By calling as much as he did, she knew he wasn't going to ever stop. However, she still told him to stay away.

After sitting in front of the house, he would always go back to his boy Mikey's house. Mikey started taking him, along with a few more of their friends, to the bar to ease his mind from what he was going through. Gary and his boys started hanging out at the local bar about ten miles from Mikey's house. They noticed there was a pretty decent crowd every night they got the chance to go.

On Sunday, Monday, and Wednesday evenings, they sat at the

bar taking back shots having man talk. Some nights, Gary wasn't too talkative with his boys. He would sit like he was on his own planet, but when he did talk he would talk about sports for a while as they watched the game. Then, he would talk about his wife Katrina, the wife who didn't have a problem ignoring him. A week later, he went back over there, and he asked her, "Can we talk now, Katrina?"

He was always interrupted by her telling him, "We don't have anything to discuss." That's not what he was trying to hear.

To respect Katrina, he left, but before he could make it to the car he thought about it. Then, he turned around stared her in the eyes.

"No, Katrina! I'm not going anywhere. Katrina, I just can't let you push me out your and our daughter's lives. I can't do that, and if I have to prove to you how much I love you by not letting my family go, I will."

Their eyes connected with each other. It was hard dealing with the separation. All he knew was one day he was getting her back. She was a tough, independent woman who had been hurt a bit in her family when she was an adolescent, so she was not taking any crap. He knew getting his wife back wasn't going to be as easy as 1-2-3.

When he did stop by, she always demanded that he leave right after she let him spend a little time with their daughter out front on the porch or in the yard where they sometimes played. He would leave and wave bye to her, yelling out, "I'll be back."

Every morning, Gary would drive by the house checking on her. Some days, he would sit out front until she left, knowing one day she would stop and talk to him. Even though he went over there wanting to talk to her, he knew she wouldn't want to, but that didn't stop him from trying. When he would see the lights on throughout the house, he knew she was already awake. The majority of the time he never had the courage to knock on the door, so he would just sit out front. Sometimes when he did get out the car, he would just stand close to the house. He could either hear her singing inside the shower to the music playing or just the shower running.

The thought of Katrina being naked, singing like she was happy, made him that much madder at himself. He was determined to prove to her that their love, marriage, and he was worth holding on to.

Other times, he didn't bother knocking or ringing the doorbell. He would just sit there listening to her from the outside. On one of the days, he actually stayed without leaving, and once she opened the door to leave out to begin her day, she and their daughter jumped back. She wasn't expecting him to be standing on the porch. She screamed at him, "GARY, WHAT THE HELL!!"

"Please, Katrina. Let me talk."

"No, Gary! Please leave now. Right now is not a good time for this."

"Hi, Daddy! You're back!!" Simone said happily.

"Hey, daddy's baby girl."

Simone ran up to her dad, and he picked her up hugging her.

"Daddy, I missed you."

"I missed you too," he told her.

"Daddy, are you still out working, or you staying home now?"

He looked at Katrina before answering their daughter. Katrina turned her head to avoid looking at him.

"Baby, daddy is still out working."

"Yeah, and he has to leave already, so give your daddy a kiss bye," Katrina told her. Simone then kissed her dad, and he put her down.

Gary turned around and left. After he pulled off, she did too. Gary didn't quite leave like she thought he did. She was not paying attention to anything besides what was in front of her and the music she was singing to on the FM radio Power 106. Gary just drove around the corner and pulled around to see her pass. Once she passed him, he waited a few seconds and began driving slowly to follow her from a long distance.

He followed her the whole time, popping up at all the houses she was showing. He was still trying to talk. Katrina was so embarrassed by him doing that in front of her clients. After the fourth house, she just went off on him. He finally got the picture. Then, he left.

Chris and Brandy were also going through their situations too. It didn't matter to her that he no longer wanted to get married to her as long as she was able to wake up every morning with him and go to sleep every night with him.

Although she wanted more, she knew she was the reason why his mind had not changed. She was going to stick by him like he demonstrated to her. She loved him and was not going to give up. She just hoped in the future his mind would change. She had something to prove to Chris, and she wasn't going to stop until she did.

Chapter 9

Let Me Explain

The next day, Gary decided to go see Katrina unexpectedly. On the drive to their house, Gary rehearsed what and how he was going to say what he was about to say. After a few knocks on the door, Katrina opened it, but she stood blocking the entrance of the door. The first thing she said was, "How are you going to come over here without calling to make sure it's okay?"

"I need to talk to you about something."

She was fixing her lips to say something, but then he stopped and told her, "Please, don't say a word. Let me explain."

She leaned against the front door and listened to him talk while waiting for her turn. They took turns back and forth with their feedback to each other. He had a reason for whatever she came at him with. She was stunned. She still wasn't changing her mind; she still didn't want anything to do with him by the time they were done with the back and forth.

He was a little confused because it seemed she was having some sort of understanding by nodding her head when he said certain things. She was feeling insulted as his wife when all he had to do was come talk to her.

"So, you fucked my sister!!? And you think that's excusable?"

That shot him down. He froze staring at her and forgot everything he was about to say. Then, he had to raise his voice at her, telling her to calm down, but she wouldn't.

"Huh, Huh!!" her voice sounded. When she asked him, it took him a few moments to even reply.

"Yes, but baby, it had been a while since you showed me some attention in the bed you know."

She gave him the coldest look. In so many words, he tried to defend what he had done. She wasn't buying it. He knew damn well what he was doing.

"Baby, you came home tired from working all day, and all you wanted to do was clean up and cook us dinner. Baby, I needed sex."

"WHAT!!" She just couldn't believe the shit he was saying.

He was saying the same thing over again. Katrina started to break down. He stood there seeing her broken down from how badly he had hurt her by cheating on her. But through it all, he never stopped loving her and thinking about her. He tried stepping closer to her to hug her. But she threw her arm out to indicate she didn't need his hug.

"So, what you go fuck my baby sister?" Not once had she paid any attention to how unhappy he was about not getting sex every single day and night back then.

"Babe, I didn't even think you loved me anymore," he said. "Baby, you even stopped being intimate as much. I didn't know what was going on."

"Really, Gary!!" she said with her squinted eyes staring at him.

"So, you go fuck my sister while she was sleeping? Gary, just because it was not every single day didn't not mean I didn't love you. Did you ever stop to think I was just tired from working all day?"

"I'm sorry, babe," he said with the look of 'I'm really sorry' in his eyes.

"You are probably still fucking her, huh?"

"No, babe," he said. "I've been crashing out at Mikey's house. At first, I was at a hotel for a while, but I couldn't take that shit anymore, so I called my boy. Off that, babe. I need you. Baby, I need you. I miss you. I want my family back. I can barely breathe without you and Simone. I know I fucked up. I shouldn't have done some of the things I did, but I'm sorry. I just wasn't thinking."

Staring into his eyes, Katrina could tell he meant every bit of the words he said.

She asked, "So what, Gary, does Mikey do the same thing to his wife?"

"No, baby," he said. "He and his wife are just letting me rent out one of their rooms for a little of nothing until we patch things up."

"I know his wife Chevon would not accept that shit from him. So why do this to me, Gary?" She didn't want to discuss it anymore, so she slammed the door in his face. Gary had said a little bit more than what Katrina wanted to hear.

"KATRINA, OPEN THE DOOR!!" he shouted. "Baby, open

up!! Gary shouted again from on the other side of the closed door. At that point, Katrina was done talking, but not once had she screamed divorce. That is how he knew he still had a chance. "Baby, we can fix this!!" he shouted.

Gary continued talking loudly, screaming on the other side of the door. He didn't care who heard him or what neighbors were looking or listening. He was trying to get his wife back.

"Baby!! What about everything we have?" he shouted. "Baby, Katrina! Open the door. I'm sorry. I wasn't trying to upset you. I was just trying to explain the situation of what happened."

She never did open the door again. He left and went back to his boy Mikey's house. Despite Gary's actions and what he did to her, she still was the bigger person when it came down to him seeing and talking to their daughter.

Chapter 10

Reunited

Almost a year later, Katrina called Gary. Gary answered his phone sounding as though he was asleep. Katrina looked up at the clock to see what time it was. It was only six o'clock in the evening.

"Hello, Gary. Oh, I'm sorry. Gary, did I catch you at a bad time?" she asked. He quickly began to wake up after hearing her voice. He was shocked she had called him. He looked down at his phone to see if it was really her name on the caller ID. When he saw her name, his eyes opened more.

"Oh no, baby. It's never a bad time. You can call me any time. No matter what, I will always answer your call."

"How are you?" she asked.

"I'm wonderful now that I hear your voice."

"It's been a while."

"Yeah, it has."

Katrina didn't waste any time and straight out told him, "Well the reason I called is because Simone misses her daddy being here at the house." Before she called him, she had already been on his mind; his family was all he could think about.

The conversation was going nicely and pleasant between them. Katrina and Gary began talking about reuniting for the sake of their daughter. Simone wanted to see her dad daily like she had before. But Katrina did not love him the same since they separated because she was so hurt after she found out he was fucking her sister.

But Simone loved her dad and was too young to know what was going on. Katrina never wanted to hurt her daughter behind what had being going on between them. She always wanted her daughter to feel loved and happy and not as though she was in an unstable and unloving household.

Putting her daughter first is what Katrina did. She knew it would be best to get over the past and forgive her husband. That is why she called Gary and told him he could come back home, but she had to inhale and exhale quite a bit before she called. Katrina thought she would think of her daughter's feelings that time instead of her own. Thinking and praying silently, she hoped she was making the right decision.

Gary was shocked the conversation was going the way it was. The conversation continued.

"Gary, I was wondering if you are not involved with anyone if you want to come back home."

He immediately began to let her know he knew he had messed up big time and being away from his family for all those years had taught him a lesson. He promised to never hurt her again, nor think about ever doing something stupid again.

"I love you, Katrina! I love my daughter. I missed my baby girl

Simone. I owe you both the biggest apology in the world. I am so so sorry," he told her.

She wasn't so sure of him at first because of what he had already done to her, but after hearing how serious he sounded, she knew he was for real. She felt there was no need for any marital counseling to get their marriage strong again. She already knew what they needed to start doing in order for them to be okay again.

She said to him, "Hey, why don't we raise our daughter together?" He thought he would never hear those words again nor be under the same roof again. He was excited. After Katrina said what she had to say, he was happy and in shock that the day he had been waiting for was now there. He definitely was looking forward to seeing her.

After talking to Gary and hearing he still felt the same way about her, she contacted her phone provider to have them change her number. She respected him, and she didn't want to cause any trouble. But, the way she was starting to feel for Mike wouldn't let her come out and tell him, "Hey Mike, I'm getting back with my husband." She just couldn't say those words.

Her coming together with her husband to raise their daughter Simone in a two-parent household was the right thing to do. But, loving Gary the same as she had before was going to take her some time to do.

The moment she heard the doorbell ring, she quickly turned the oven off. Dinner was ready. Katrina quickly ran over to the door to answer it. Upon his entry, she stood still. He walked in and hugged her. They both enjoyed the moment, as they stood still in the same spot hugging each other tightly. He cried softly over her shoulder. She knew he would tear up, because he was an emotional kind of guy, but only when someone hurt him emotionally.

At that very moment, old memories surfaced in his mind of what his daughter had told him in the past about Katrina's friend Mike. The thought of another man who was probably having sex with his wife or just being with his wife was hurtful. It was hitting him. *I fucked up*, he thought as he shook his head. *This was all from my own behavior*, was all he could tell himself. Tears continued to run down his face, before she could even have him sit at the dinner table.

His first night back in the house, Katrina prepared fried pork chops, made macaroni 'n cheese, cabbage, homemade yams and sweet cornbread. Before their daughter Simone came to the dinner table, Katrina passed him a damp towel to wipe his face. They missed eating as a family while talking and laughing. Neither Katrina nor Gary wanted their daughter to know they had been having problems within their marriage for the past few years. So, they just told her he was out of town working a lot of long hours, and sometimes his job required him to go out of state.

Noticing her wedding ring was off her finger and how dark that area of her finger was, he could tell she hadn't wore it in a while. After dinner, Simone gave her parents a kiss and went to bed. Then,

Katrina and Gary went to bed also. Katrina went straight to her closet and picked out one of her sexy gowns to wear. Then, she went into the bathroom that was in their room and changed to get comfortable for bed. While Katrina was inside the bathroom changing, Gary saw no need to wait until she came back for him to change. So, he took off his clothes leaving nothing but his boxer shorts. When Katrina came out, he was laid back in the bed watching her hips with her every move as she walked towards him. She couldn't help but stare at his muscular chest that she missed rubbing. Katrina got in bed and lay close to him, and Gary began to rub his hand up her arm as they talked. He missed feeling her soft skin, the way her body felt and just being with his beautiful wife. It was all because he was thinking with the wrong head that left him by himself. She missed how his hands could make her feel and how they soothed her body. Instantly, his rubbing made her get warm between her legs.

Laying over her with his head against her chest while listening to her heart beat and rubbing the side of his face against her cream colored lace gown turned him on. Through her lingerie, he could see her hard, pointed nipples. He couldn't keep his eyes off. He wanted to rub them, but he knew if he were to rub them, he was going to have sex next. That night he didn't want to think of sex though she made it hard not too from what she had chosen to wear to bed. He didn't want to come back like that. Just being under her and focusing on what he missed was enough. He didn't even bother unpacking that night.

They just stayed in the bed talking all night long about what they had been doing for the years they had been separated and their future plans. Never once did they speak of the past and the issues that had occurred with Brandy. They both made an agreement to start fresh as if it didn't happen. Gary spent the night holding her tightly, kissing her, and talking. He was being romantic and so sweet, like he always was. And, they realized how much they had missed each other. Finally, they both fell asleep. Deep down inside, Katrina loved him still.

Katrina knew he was and had always been a good man that gave her the world, even before they got engaged and married. He took really good care of her and truly loved her and their daughter Simone.

When they woke up, they glanced out the window and saw how beautiful the day was. The sun colored the sky with light. That morning, Gary woke up still on hard. It was pretty hard for him not to want to do some freaky things to his wife, but he made it through. But from there on out, he vowed to remain a man of his word. He told her he would wait until she was ready. She saw his arousal, but she didn't say anything about it. Still thinking about it from time to time, she just knew she would regret letting her sister stay with them. They thought their life were perfect until their little visitor showed up. Not to mention him not being able to get sexual affection every single night like he wanted.

Everything else between them was so perfect. She sat beside him thinking. Everything about her seemed different, from the way she walked to the way she talked. It was like her whole attitude changed in a good way. Katrina was happy to have him back. But after six months of being back together, something inside her caused her to find herself still unhappy about her marriage.

She wanted to see if things would eventually change the way she was feeling. Katrina wasn't sure if she was ready to give up yet on Gary. By the ninth month, the guilt for leaving Mike the way she did was hanging over her head. The way she changed her number on him like that was kicking her in her butt. She thought about how she really liked him. He was the type who remembered birthdays: hers and even her daughter's, the personal appointments, and any type of special occasion. He had always enjoyed spending time with her and Simone all in that short time she had known him.

Once she got the chance to call him, she did let him know she had gotten back together with her husband and was trying to work out the family thing.

He said, "Let me," then he stopped talking.

"Let you what?" she asked Mike.

"Let me be the one to love you and be the man you need in your life."

Silence was all they heard on the phone after he said that, while he waited for the response he wanted to hear.

She said, "I'm sorry. I want to try and hang on to my marriage," and then she hung up.

Katrina wasn't trying to be rude to him, but she knew if she didn't hang up on him she probably would have given in. Katrina took a deep breath after getting that off her chest. Now she could focus on Gary, herself and their daughter without the guilt of dealing with another man and hiding it in the back of her head.

Damn... she thought. What he said just hit her. She didn't know he felt like that for her. *Katrina, you have to focus here,* she said to herself.

Katrina never once meant for the intimacy in their marriage to have ever slowed down from being too tired from working. If he would have come to her and ignored her being fussy from being too tired and just sat her down in front of him and talked to her about what he really wanted, she wouldn't have had a choice but to sit there and listen. Then, she would have seen how seriously he wanted it.

Over time, they rebuilt their friendship and relationship. Never did he expect for her to believe in and trust him in the beginning. He was just more satisfied that she let him back in and was giving him a chance to be a better person with better judgment. Gary didn't think what he thought would be a once-in-a-while quickie was going to turn into a yearlong affair and a baby.

It had been almost nine months since Gary had been back with Katrina and still she hadn't gave him any sex. She was still hurt, and rebuilding the trust was slow. He expected that because he knew he messed up big time by what he had done. Even though he didn't know she was going to take as long as she had before giving him any. He just decided having an affair wasn't worth it and realized it was very stupid on his part. He was just going to wait until she was comfortable and ready again. He hoped she had erased his and her sister's affair out her head, so he could have his wife back like he had at the beginning of their marriage.

Being selfish and not just thinking of himself is what he planned not to do anymore. Being inconsiderate and not fulfilling his every need is something she planned not to ever do again.

It had taken a whole year before Katrina had decided to put the past behind them. But when she did, she was for sure ready to get intimate. When she did turn time into intimate time to share with him, it was the moans he had missed; he missed hearing the sounds of her screaming out his name. That Wednesday night, after both of them had a very long day at work and going to Parent/Teacher night at their daughter's school, they were ready for some alone time. After sending their daughter to bed, after she was done with her dinner and bath, they went to their room and closed and locked their door. Their clothes came off, and they took a shower together, washing each other's body. Once they finished, they got out and dried off and went straight for their bed. He laid her back on the bed raising her legs up a little while spreading them wide open. He licked her until she was wet down there, so he could have it easy when he slid it in.

Gary licked her for a while until she couldn't take it. They began to make love while looking deeply into each other's eyes. They almost didn't blink. They were both moaning, and she was screaming out his name. The moment his tongue touched her lips kissing her, her whole body tingled. She hadn't felt like that since she could remember. Shortly they released each other lips to remember their last time. Gary wasn't ready to cum yet, so he stopped for a moment, letting it stay inside. They talked about when they last made love and how it was breathtaking. They were both ready to take each other's breath all night long. As the passions were moving through their bodies, he started moving in deeply again, and they couldn't stop kissing. They were enjoying themselves so much.

As he went in and out of her, he could feel her tighten her clitoris. She loved doing that. She knew he could feel it tighten up on his penis, and he always loved when she did it. She felt as though she was sinking in deeper and deeper with every hard push into their pillow-top mattress. The sensations moving through their bodies made them feel all over again how they both felt when it was their first time, and why they fell in love and got married twelve years ago.

After the sexual pleasure they had, they were both energized. They looked at the time, and it was already three o'clock in the morning. They got out of bed and started making breakfast together in the kitchen. By the time Simone got dressed and ready for school, Katrina had re-warmed the food, and Simone went to the table and joined them before it was time for her to go. They decided to take the day off from work and spend it together doing nothing. They drove Simone to school.

Getting out the car, Simone was happy and waving bye to her parents. On the way home, they did a little window shopping at the plaza near their home. When they got home, they both went to the room and passed out on the bed; they were tired. Two o'clock that afternoon the alarm was set to wake them up to pick up their daughter, but instead her phone rang just two minutes before it was set to wake them up. It was like she was being timed, like whoever it was calling knew she was about to wake up. She knew it could only be Shante, Sharee, her mother, or a potential client. Looking down at her screen, it was her mother. She placed the call on speaker as they got ready to leave to pick up their daughter from school.

Deborah, Katrina's mother, was calling to tell her there was a family gathering scheduled for the next week at her aunt Lucy's house for her cousin Edward. The gathering would start at 5pm, and she wanted her to come. Edward was Katrina and Brandy's cousin, and he was coming home for a week from the military.

Katrina hadn't seen all her family at one time since her niece Paige's birthday. She couldn't imagine what everyone was going to think seeing her back with him. She didn't know if she was quite ready to be seen in the presence of her family with him right then.

"Hi, Mom!" Gary said.

"Hello, son. You okay? How have you been?"

"Better now," he shouted.

"Well son, I'm glad to hear that. Well now, I want to see you too at your aunt Lucy's house for the gathering next week.

"We will be there," they said.

"How is my grandbaby?"

"She's fine. We are about to go and pick her up from school now," Katrina told her.

"Have her give her granny a call once she gets home."

"Okay, Mom."

"Oh, baby, my other line is clicking. I'm going to go now. It's my friend Bernice."

"Love you, Mom," they shouted out.

"Oh, Katrina, behave. Your sister might be there, okay?"

"Yes, Mom. I will behave," then they hung up.

Promising not to bring any drama to the party, she knew her mother was going to hold her to that. She told herself she was just going to go next week and try not to care what anyone had to say.

The evening of the party Katrina, Gary and Simone made it on time; they pulled up at five. When her great aunts say five o'clock, that's what they mean. No "CP" time with them. Arriving to Aunt Lucy's house that evening, Katrina was hoping they made it before her thousands of cousins did just to get a close enough parking spot. She didn't want to have to walk far in her heels. Just six houses down from her aunt's, they could already hear the music. By the loudness of the music, she could hear the fun had already got started.

Walking up her stairs, they began to look at each other giving the google eye look as they grinned and laughed with a smirk, with worries of how the night for them was about to turn out. As they went inside, everyone spoke and said hi with smiles, as they walked through and gave everyone a peck on their cheeks and a hug. They all seemed happy to see Gary and Katrina. Joining in with the family is what she always enjoyed and something she had always cherished.

Katrina was surprised no one had anything bad to say. After all, no one is perfect. Being at Aunt Lucy's house brought back her good childhood memories of growing up when their family used to have a family gathering every single holiday or just because they enjoyed coming together having cook outs. That's what they did back then. She missed those good old days.

Walking through the house, she didn't see her mother yet, but she knew she was there already because she saw her car outside. Katrina knew just where to find her- IN THE KITCHEN. Yes, that's where she was.

"Hey, Ma," they gave her mother a hug and a kiss, along with her grandbaby. They walked around the island towards Aunt Lucy to give her a hug and kiss as well.

"Hey, baby. How are you?" Aunt Lucy said with much expression and a smile. Aunt Lucy wiped her hands on her apron and gave Katrina, Gary, and Simone a hug and kiss. "I'm fine. We're fine. Look at you, Aunt Lucy. You're looking good, Aunt Lucy."

"Aww. Thank you, baby."

"Yeah, I like your dress." Katrina looked at her mother and said, "Momma, look at Aunt Lucy looking fly over here."

Next, they both headed for her grandmother, "Grandmother Estella." She was sixty-five, and Katrina loved her to death. She was the one to tell it like it is with no filter from her brain to her mouth. She didn't care. She always said, "It's better to tell the truth. Why sugar coat? Just be real."

Surprisingly, she didn't say anything as Katrina and Gary gave her a hug. All she did was shake her head and smile. Katrina knew she wanted to say something, but she didn't. That wasn't like her. Normally, she wouldn't hold anything in, but knowing her grandmother, she knew she was about to say something at any moment. Katrina told Gary he could go in the front room with the men while she helped out in the kitchen a bit. Gary gave her a kiss as he went to the front room with everyone else.

Katrina looked at her mother, then back at her grandmother. Once again, she shook her head and said, "I'm going to let you make your own decision on this. Just let it be the best decision for you, baby."

"This is about taking him back huh?" Her granny just looked at her. "Well, Granny. I thought I was doing the right thing for Simone. She missed her daddy."

"Something like that you have to do it for you, not no one else, not even for Simone," her granny told her. Katrina loved her grandmother to death and valued her every opinion. That statement alone made Katrina think.

Katrina's mother blurted out and said, "Baby, as long as you are happy, things are going to work themselves out."

"Well, if I have to remind you, he did have a baby with your sister."

"Hush, Mom!" Deborah looked over and told her mom. Katrina stood with a blank look on her face.

Estella looked at her grandbaby, then at her daughter. "Look at her, Deborah." Deborah looked at Katrina and seeing the look on her face, she asked her mom to stop it already. "Okay, I'll keep quiet now," her mother said to her.

Katrina's mother stepped in between them and said, "Katrina, baby go on and enjoy the party."

Katrina took two platters of deviled eggs out the fridge and took them into the living room. As she walked in, Edward also walked in and said, "Hey, family! I'm home!" Everyone was so happy to see him, and he was just as happy to see them as well.

"It's so wonderful to see you, cousin!!" Katrina shouted with a smile. He made his way to hug every member in his family. Everyone began engaging in conversation with him. Katrina quickly placed the platters on the table and went back into the kitchen to get drinks to take out there. But before leaving from the kitchen, her granny called her over and gave her a hug.

As she hugged her, she whispered into Katrina's ear and told her she loved her and that she needed to do what was right for her and no one else, and if being with him still made her happy, then she was happy for her. Katrina gave her granny a hug, and then she went back into the living room taking more food and drinks. She went and kissed her husband and began enjoying the party along with everyone else.

What is Marriage?

A marriage begins when vows are exchanged; vows are promises made to each other during a wedding ceremony, and any problem the two should have, they are supposed to work it out together as one until things are back how the two want it to be.

Marriage is supposed to take each other for richer or poorer, for better or worse, in sickness and health, forsaking all others until death do them part.

Marriage is a lifelong commitment. There is more to marriage than love and sex. It is a partnership that one has to patient in and work hard to keep. You must both have a lot of trust, respect and loyalty for one another and be each other's backbone in any and everything, including managing finances for everything.

Communicate daily and be honest about the needs of each other and be always willing to fulfill them.

A Message

I was excited while writing this book but even more excited to finish it. I hoped you found my novel enjoyable to read just as I did with the crazy drama, secrets, the sex and steamy love scenes.

It's a story you have probably heard before from a friend or two or maybe you yourself were involved in something similar with a similar outcome *or not*.

Now that you have read this book, I hope I spoke to you in some way through the black ink on the pages.

Epilogue
Secret Love

Even if Katrina would have had the chance to think about what she should have or could have done before her husband slept with her sister, it still didn't give him the right to sleep with her sister or any other person besides her. Communication would have been best.

After years of separation from him, while he pleaded and begged for her to allow him to come back the whole time, she gave in after five years. That didn't make her seem like a fool at all. After a period of time of having fun with the girls, taking care of her daughter by herself and just living life responsibly really gave her a lot of time to think and understand no one's perfect. We all make mistakes, and we must learn from them to better ourselves. But after the second and third mistake, the person giving in is made…the fool.

With another person, things could be worse. People think the grass is greener on the other side, but patching things up and making it the way you want is sometimes all you need to do.

After a year of being back together, Katrina and Gary's marriage was nothing more than raising together their daughter Simone in a loving and stable two-parent household. For Katrina and Gary, that's what worked for them. However, they still tried hard to rebuild what they had and to not make any of the same mistakes. It had taken time, and it was a process.

After that year, for a different reason something wasn't clicking: When Gary arrived home and saw a car in front of the house, he asked, "Whose car is this?" as he drove along the side of it looking inside to see if anyone was inside. No one, of course, was there. When he walked inside to ask Katrina whose car was outside, he heard an unexpected voice behind him…………………..

Stay Tuned for Secret Love 2

Dear Readers,

Stay tuned for other books coming soon. And you can, if you would, join me on my Facebook page "SecretLove Book," so you can be informed of all my latest releases.

I hope you enjoyed this first book. I loved creating the characters, and I hope you enjoyed them too.

Coming Soon:

Having *It* His *Way*

I Have More

About the Author

My Point of View

Reading Group Questions

About the Author

LaShane Moore likes to keep busy writing books every day. She finds it hard to put the pen down. Writing is her enjoyment, and it is how she relaxes. She is a full-time mom, with a full-time job, who write novels part-time. With her busy schedule, she is watching it all pay off, as that is what she enjoys seeing.

She is living proof that you can do whatever you set your heart to do. Even when you think you can't, "You Can."

Her desire is to keep the books coming with the "I don't want to put the book down" type of books, filled with real-life situations to inspire and motivate and also to entertain with a good read.

My Point of View

I wrote this book because number one, it's too many secrets and hidden agendas in these relationships. I wanted to reveal in detail the different things I did, far as my characters motives, actions, and their thoughts through them (my characters), so that way my readers could either see themselves or be helpful to someone who's blind to their own situation. It's funny how some people could always see what's going on in everyone else situation but not their own. Some people are the cause to their own situation and don't even realize it, and that things could still of had hope and changed for the better and sometimes all it take is one or a few minor changes. I figure letting my readers not only read something very entertaining with the juicy drama, love, romance, and detailed erotic scenes but a novel that could be an eye opener, a novel that could do both inspire and motivate as well. I figured letting my readers into the head of my characters was something important. I want my novel to be a reason someone life has changed for the better, or someone marriage took a turn for greatness and happiness. We have way too many broken marriages, what happened to, til due us part. To many men or women not being loyal and sleeping around. I wanted my novel to make my readers love more, not just saying it but actually showing it and meaning it. I wanted my novel to help my readers communicate with understanding with their husband or wife or their boyfriend or girlfriend. I put my all into this first novel of mines and I hoped you enjoyed reading my Secret Love-In the beginning novel. It is a series so this means after you leave me a book review on amazon then part two is waiting for you to purchase. Thank you once again for reading my Secret Love Novel. Enjoy part two.

Reading Group Questions

1. Katrina made a decision to let her sister move in with her and her husband. Even though she changed her hoorish way far as sleeping with any and every one for money, do you think she was crazy for allowing her sister to move in?

2. Gary didn't care about his consequences when he began to have his affair with his wife sister, so why is he begging his now to let him in. Do you think Katrina was wrong for putting him out or do you think she knew what she was getting herself into when she allowed her sister to move in?

3. To of what extent do you think Brandy was wrong for not saying anything to her sister? Remember her sister husband Gary was the one who sled inside of her while she was asleep.

4. Do you recognize any of these situations in this Novel that may have happened to you or someone

you know? If so, NOW WHAT ARE YOU GOING TO DO is the question?

5. What does Brandy character adds to this novel?

6. What does Gary character adds to this novel?

7. What does Katrina character adds to this novel?

8. What was the importance of consistency and understanding in this novel?

9. How do you feel about what Brandy did to Chris? Remember he thought he was with a woman who was loyal to him like he was to her, he didn't know she was sleeping and having an affair with her sister husband and had a baby by him and made him think the baby was his.

10. Was Chris crazy to stay with Brandy after finding out the truth about the baby not being his? It's not the child fault and he already grew an attachment. Remember he thought the child was his.

11. At the end do you think Katrina was stupid for reaching out to her husband? It's not wrong to try and fix a broken marriage or is it? Some marriages could be fixed.

12. Did Katrina bring the trouble into her marriage thinking her sister was changed and that she wouldn't dare to do anything in such nature? Does the blame only falls on her husband Gary? All he wanted was sex every night he was horny.